Threads

From The Chicken House

I still love dressing up. Funny old clothes, smart
new ones and that old hat from a junk shop in
Ireland that I adore. But in Sophia Bennett's
prize-winning book, fashion is not only about
feeling good – it's art, it's freedom, it means
doing something that changes lives in all kinds of
ways. *Threads* is brilliant, funny, heartwarming
and *creative*. Like my old hat.

Barry Cunningham
Publisher

SOPHIA BENNETT

Threads

2 Palmer Street, Frome, Somerset BA11 1DS

Text © Sophia Bennett 2009
First published in Great Britain in 2009
The Chicken House
2 Palmer Street
Frome, Somerset BA11 1DS
United Kingdom
www.doublecluck.com

Cover design and interior design by Tracey Paris
Typeset by Dorchester Typesetting Group Ltd
Printed and bound in Great Britain by CPI Bookmarque, CR0 4TD

The paper used in this Chicken House book is made from wood grown in sustainable forests.

1 3 5 7 9 10 8 6 4 2

British Library Cataloguing in Publication data available.

ISBN 978-1-905294-98-5

*To Emily, Sophie, Freddie and Tom
and Alex, for making it all possible
and Noney, for her joy in beautiful things*

Chapter 1

*W*e're standing in a fashion designer's studio in Hoxton, admiring ourselves in the mirror. At least, Jenny's supposed to be admiring herself in her red-carpet dress. Or she would if it didn't make her look like a cherry tomato. Edie and I are just tagging along, but the mirror takes up the whole wall and it's hard not to take a bit of a peek.

Apart from the mirror, the studio's big and bare. Lots of brick walls and tall windows and clothes rails. My mother would call it 'industrial chic'. I would say it was in need of some love and upholstery.

I'm looking at my Converses, which got their first outing today after a bit of customisation with some Tipp-Ex. They're only mild French swear-words (and one in Italian that I got from my pen pal, Marco). I know much worse ones. I thought they were funny and Jenny laughed. Edie is above such things. But Mum this morning when I came downstairs in them . . . well, you wouldn't think she'd been a model and walked HALF NAKED down a catwalk in her time. She wants me to be preppy and brainy like Edie and have the youth she never had. I quite like the sound of the youth she did have.

I'm not so sure about my silver leggings, although they're gorgeous. They seemed slinky and alluring in my bedroom, but under the studio lights I look as if I'm about to blast off. The velvet top is cute, though. It used to be a dress, but works so much better without the sleeves and skirt. And the black lace fingerless gloves were a definite find. I'm quite pleased with the overall effect.

Edie's trying to pretend she's not looking at herself. She has a model's body (I don't; I take after my father, who's French and smokes Gitanes and is practically a midget), but she dresses it in knee-length skirts and Kate Middleton jackets. Yawn yawn. She could probably do catalogues after we leave school but no: she wants to join the United Nations. Mum is SO impressed.

Edie's surreptitiously looking at her face. She's pretty in a blonde, centre-parting sort of way. You can't see her brains behind those steel-grey eyes. She's trying to work out whether she should get a fringe. She's been thinking about this for the last five years and no decision yet. She catches me watching her and makes out she's admiring Jenny, which is a total giveaway.

Jenny is un-admirable right now. A lovely person and my best friend, but THAT DRESS. It does nothing for her. And to think she has to wear it to a premiere in a week.

Jenny's done a lot of things over the last year and a half. She's turned from a bouncy, freckly, funny twelve-year-old into a totally new edition. For a start, she's grown boobs and developed an interesting line in facial spots. She's acted in an action movie with Hollywood's Hottest Couple and the New Teenage Sex God – not something you want to be doing with the whole boob/spot thing going on. And she's developed a complex about her weight.

If we lived fifty years ago, she'd be hot. She's probably the same size and shape as Marilyn Monroe. But in today's Size Zero age, she thinks she's fat. She's embarrassed about the boobs. Mine are way behind and Edie will forever have fried eggs. She's even embarrassed about her skin, which blushes easily. She hates her freckles and her copper hair. She really just wants to disappear.

But she's not going to do it in that cherry tomato number. The designer's called Pablo Dodo. Don't try and remember his name, because if he's always this rubbish, he's likely to become extinct. He's the cousin of one of the movie's producers, which is how he got the job. He wanted to turn Jenny into 'a vision in red'. Which shows the limit of his imagination. Between her hair and her blushes, she can do that all by herself.

Last time she came, Jenny told Pablo about her boob phobia and he promised to hide them. This he has done.

They're buried somewhere under the crimson, floaty, chiffon number that starts at her collarbone and continues outwards down to her mid-thigh, before stopping suddenly, as if it's remembered something, leaving her pinky-white legs somewhat stranded.

I'm trying to think of something to say, which is normally not difficult for me, but right now I'm challenged. Edie is biting her lip.

Pablo's assistant is organising the final fitting. She comes over, mouth full of pins, and starts adjusting, muttering about the 'cheerful brightness' of the chiffon.

'What do you think, Nonie?' Jenny asks me, slipping her feet into a pair of gold stilettos. She looks anxious and unsure (although she'd go well with a rocket salad).

I smile encouragingly, but stay silent. I'm picturing that red-carpet moment and it hurts.

Edie can't hold it in any more.

'You look like a cherry tomato,' she gasps at last. 'In heels.'

And she's the one who wants to be a diplomat.

Ten minutes later, after some pinning and shifting about behind a tatty old curtain, Jenny re-emerges in her jeans and tee-shirt uniform, looking squashed. I have tried to explain that cut-offs and a shirt tied at the midriff à la Marilyn would look fantastic on her, but she's too depressed to listen.

I've given Edie the Look, but she just shrugged at me.

She believes in honesty between friends. And she's too busy being super-intelligent to notice the consequences.

Thanks to Edie, we have to rush for the Tube to get back across London. She volunteers with special needs children on Saturday afternoons. Edie's entire life is organised around getting CV points for her application to Harvard in three years' time. You're supposed to go there before you join the UN, apparently. It's where Reese Witherspoon went in *Legally Blonde*. I seem to remember that in the movie Reese made a video of herself by the pool and the Harvard professors let her in. Edie makes it look *much* more complicated. And not only because pools are hard to come by in London.

Meanwhile, I've promised to treat Jenny to a smoothie at the Victoria and Albert Museum (the V&A to its friends), which is round the corner from my house. It's the coolest venue in London, with the chicest café – full of vintage tiles and crazy lights the size of space-hoppers – and the best smoothies I've tasted, after years of market research.

It's Jenny's last chance to do something normal before the promotion tour for her new movie goes hyper. The London premiere's next Saturday. Before that there are press interviews, TV interviews and photocalls. Then afterwards, more interviews. Then a trip to New York, LA and Japan to do it all over again.

Pablo Dodo says he sees her as a vision in pink for the New York premiere. God help us all.

Chapter 2

On the way to the Tube, a couple of men in dirty denim jackets and jeans shout across to us from the other side of the street.

'Weirdo.'

'Get a life, silver legs.'

Edie puts a protective arm around me and Jenny holds my hand, but I'm used to it. I don't really mind any more. When some drop-dead fashion god rubbishes the way I look, I might be mildly upset, but guys in head-to-toe denim aren't really in a position to criticise.

Edie tries to change the subject. Sort of.

'You should see the girl I'm working with this afternoon,' she announces. 'She's *seriously* weird. She goes through different phases but at the moment she's into ballet tutus and fairy wings. I mean, fine if you're five, but she's twelve. I never know what to expect next with her. If she shows up at all, that is. She's missed the last two sessions and she's in mega-trouble if she misses this one.'

'What are you doing with her?' Jenny asks.

'Reading. She's dyslexic. Seriously dyslexic. Her brain just isn't wired up for spelling. Last time we were working on "chair". I have to give her reading strategies.'

Jenny and I have no idea what reading strategies are, but decide not to ask. Edie's quite capable of spending the whole journey telling us.

On the train, she gets some books out of her bag and shows us what she's brought to tempt the girl with this week. They're all stories about small children and animals, with big letters and no word over two syllables. Then she pulls out the Jane Austen she's in the middle of and settles down with it. Knowing her, she'll have finished it by this evening.

Jenny and I get to South Kensington station and bid her goodbye. The V&A is a short walk away in the early summer sunshine. I love it. The buildings are large and chunky and colourful and rambling. You could get lost in them for days. As always, we go through the costume section to get to the café, so I can get my fix of inspirational outfits.

Today, I'm busy admiring a John Galliano wedding dress when Jenny grabs my hand and yanks it.

'Ow!'

'Look!' she whispers so loudly she might as well shout it.

'What?'

She starts to giggle. 'I think Edie's going to be out of luck today.'

I follow the line of her stare. Sitting in front of my favourite cabinet – the one with the eighteenth-century embroidered court dress – is a little black girl with a satchel and a notebook, who's busy sketching. I see what Jenny means. The girl is wearing blue cotton dungarees, but they're swamped by an oversize pink practice tutu and there's a tattered pair of pink fairy wings slung over her shoulders. She's topped it all off with a sky-blue crotchet beret scattered with beads and fake pearls. London is a trendy fashion capital, but even so, this outfit is distinctive.

She's staring intently at what she's doing and doesn't notice us.

'Should we say something?' Jenny asks.

I shake my head. 'Not our problem.'

'But Edie mentioned mega-trouble.'

'We can't go up to some stranger and say she needs to be in reading practice. She'd think we were nuts.'

'She's not exactly super-normal.'

I take this as a personal insult. People who choose to dress differently from the crowd should not be labelled and judged, in my opinion. I sniff in an offended sort of way and walk off. Jenny rushes after me.

'Sorry, Nonie. I didn't mean . . . You know what I meant.'

* * *

In the café, we drink our smoothies in silence. I'm trying to look hurt, still, but actually I'm feeling guilty. Jenny's probably right. The girl will be due for some dire punishment and we probably should have helped her. I'm just not as brave about these things as Jenny.

Jenny's looking anxious again. In the end, I give in and ask her what the problem is.

'Nothing. Just . . . thinking about next week, that's all.'

I feel guiltier still. This is supposed to be a cheering-up day, before all the interviews and publicity and being on her best behaviour.

Some fourteen-year-olds would be itching to live the Hannah Montana life and be on a red carpet beside Hollywood's Hottest Couple and sexy, seventeen, green-eyed Joe Yule (Joe Drool to the press and the rest of his adoring public). Not Jenny. She seems to be particularly dreading her big moment and we're not making it any easier.

At least her father will be there to keep her company. This is the father who left her mother for his second mistress/third wife when Jenny was two and didn't acknowledge her existence for FIVE YEARS, but he's been a bit friendlier recently so we're giving him a second chance.

Despite her father, who's an ex-theatre director, Jenny has wanted to be an actress since she was four. Her imitation of Simon Cowell watching an act he doesn't like on one of his talent shows is so funny it physically hurts to watch it. She also does the act in question: usually a middle-aged break-dancer or a little poppet who can't quite get the high notes. Most times we have to beg her to stop so we can catch our breath.

A couple of years ago she starred as Annie in the school musical. Our school is BIG on musicals and anything theatrical. Some of the kids go straight on to drama school. Jenny was twelve and was acting with children six years older than her. Even so, she was funnier, louder and more entertaining than any of them. It helped that the part called for a cute redhead with a big voice, but you have to have talent to get that many standing ovations.

One of the parents in the audience turned out to be a casting agent for the movies. Next thing Jenny knew, she was chatting to Hollywood's Hottest Couple beside the pool of their glamorous beachside mansion. They were on the lookout for a girl with an English accent to be Joe Yule's younger sister in their new action picture called *Kid Code*. It's an adventure about a boy from London who can decipher hieroglyphics: *The Mummy* meets *Raiders of the Lost Ark*, with a teenage hero and unfeasibly attractive parents (guess who).

So off Jenny went to Hollywood, and all around the world on location, chasing baddies, getting chased by baddies and sharing witty repartee with Joe Drool. As you do.

The trouble was, nobody thought to give her any

training in acting for the screen. She'd tell me about it in long emails, written late at night after a busy day's filming. There was hardly any time for rehearsal. You were just supposed to learn your lines and go out there and do them. And she kept on being told *not* to act. Everything she'd learnt about doing things bigger on stage she had to unlearn. For the movie camera, she had to do things smaller. The director would tell her to act with her eyes and then go crazy with frustration, shouting that her eyeballs were 'EXHAUSTING HIM WITH THEIR PERPETUAL MOTION'.

And when she wasn't acting, she said the boredom of just sitting around waiting was unbelievable. There are only so many Sudokus and Mario Kart games you can do before you start to wonder if your brain is melting.

I don't think Jenny spent a single day on that set being truly happy. And now filming is finished, every time she meets a journalist she has to say what a fantastic privilege it was to work with so many talented people and how much she's looking forward to the movie coming out.

To cheer her up, I put my smoothie aside and lie through my teeth, assuring her that the red dress will be super-amazing when she's got her hair done and her new makeup and everything. She almost believes me.

Then I get her to do a few impressions of recent talent show hopefuls. At first she refuses, but soon she can't help herself and comes up with a would-be teenage tenor who has me collapsed in giggles. We start to get funny looks from other tables and decide it's time to leave.

When we get back to the costume section, the girl in the tutu is gone.

Chapter 3

*N*ext day, the strangest thing happens.

I'm in the kitchen getting myself a drink when Mum and my brother Harry come in to talk about something. The kitchen is the place where stuff usually happens in our house. It's big, white and full of designer gadgets that we don't know how to clean. The table is Italian marble ('Don't touch it, don't sit on it, don't draw on it, and for God's sake don't spill anything on it'). The floor is limestone ('Don't touch it' blah blah blah). The walls, like the rest of the house, are covered in framed photos and paintings. It looks like a West End art gallery with a cappuccino machine. But it's actually quite homely when you get used to it.

Harry lays some photos down on the table (very carefully) for Mum to look at. Harry's five years older than me and is studying art at Central St Martins, which is THE BEST ART SCHOOL IN THE WORLD. I'd be planning to go there too, if my figures didn't look like stick men and my attempts at perspective weren't like some sort of weird 3-D puzzle. As it is, my ambition is to make tea and do the photocopying for the Olsen twins or Vivienne Westwood, but I haven't told ANYONE because it would be fashion heaven and I don't want to jinx it.

At the moment, photography is Harry's thing. Before that, it was screen printing. I don't think he's decided exactly what sort of artist he's going to be yet, but he's definitely going to be GOOD.

Harry is Mum's golden boy. I should be jealous, but I can see what she means. He is supercool, because he doesn't try. He's wearing old jeans, frayed by his bike rather than by some designer, a tee-shirt from a dodgy band he saw in a field about three years ago and flip-flops. His hair is dark brown and curly, like mine, and he keeps forgetting to get it cut, so it flops over his eyes. His voice is low and always sounds as if he's about to tell a joke.

I'm pretty sure Edie fancies him, although she won't admit it. If it wasn't for the massive age difference, and him being my BROTHER, they'd make a good couple one day, because, like Edie, he's super-kind and, unlike Edie, he's also quite charming so he might balance out her diplomacy malfunctions.

Harry takes after Mum, who is still beautiful, even after all these years. She has that bone structure thing that models have ('Cheekbones, darling. What a pity you got your father's'), and smooth skin and lips that look as though they're pumped full of beeswax, but they're not. Mind you, you should see my granny – she makes Mum look positively ordinary by comparison and she's old enough to be, well, my granny.

Anyway, Harry's got the three photos laid out on the kitchen table. He needs to use one for a project he's doing and he wants Mum's opinion on which is best.

'The theme's street style,' he explains. 'I've been taking pictures of local people who've caught my eye.'

The photographs are black and white and Harry has blown them up large. He's obviously used the fancy new lens he got recently, because the foreground is sharp and the background is very blurry. He's extremely proud of that lens. I've never seen so many blurry backgrounds since he started to use it.

Anyway, we all look at the first photo, which is of a woman in a black burka, with only her eyes showing through a narrow slit in the fabric.

'I wouldn't exactly call that style,' says Mum. 'I'd call that irony. Next.'

She gives Harry a sharp look and he sheepishly pulls forward the next one. Mum starts peering at it through her glasses, but I don't even notice it because I've already spotted what's on the photo behind it.

'Watch out! Careful!'

Oh no. I realise I've spilled my drink in shock and there is water ALL OVER THE MARBLE and getting dangerously close to the burka. Harry gathers up his photos and I'm despatched for a cloth. Mum purses her lips in the way she has.

'What was *that* about?' Harry asks, crossly, when I'm done. Thank goodness it wasn't a smoothie.

'The girl in your last photo. It's just . . . I've seen her.'

'I'm not surprised,' he says casually. 'I took it near the V&A and you practically live there, don't you?'

Harry puts the photos back. Mum unpurses her lips and focuses on the last one.

'Oh, this is the best, definitely. Who is it?'

I look at it again, still shocked. The girl is resting against a railing, drawing something out of shot. There are the tutu and the fairy wings. The satchel and the note-book. They're unmistakeable. This is positively creepy.

'I don't know who she is,' I say, 'only that Edie teaches her reading. I just heard about her yesterday and now I've seen her twice. Is this some trick, Harry?'

He shakes his head and looks innocent.

'She told me her name was Crow,' he says.

'Crow what?'

'Just that. Crow. I'd love to shoot her again. She looks so tiny and fragile but there's this air of, I dunno, exuberance about her. She photographs beautifully. But she wouldn't give me her address.'

'I should think not!' Mum bursts out, horrified. 'Darling, please do *not* go around asking for the addresses of young girls. You'll get arrested. Anyway, it's a very good shot. Excellent use of natural light. Use this one.'

Mum deals in art and photography now and she's pretty successful, so what she says goes. Harry packs up the photos and I dash upstairs to call Edie and Jenny and tell them all about it.

'Spooky!'

Jenny is suitably impressed. 'It must be some sign or something.'

Edie, on the other hand, finds the whole thing perfectly logical and takes it all in her stride.

'People like that stand out,' she says calmly. 'Once you know to look out for her you'll start seeing her everywhere. It's a phenomenon.'

I take her word for it.

'Crow did show up yesterday, by the way,' she continues. 'Just in time. She was about to get loads of detentions and a letter to her guardian.'

My guilt for ignoring her yesterday washes over me again.

'You can meet her if you like. It's her school bazaar next weekend. The day of Jenny's premiere, but we'll have time for both. I promised I'd go. Crow's going to be selling some stuff she makes. And if Harry wants to see her, I'm sure he can come too.'

As I say, I've always suspected that Edie has a soft spot for my brother. I wonder whether this is just a ploy to spend an hour or two in his company. But it seems as though fate is definitely trying to get me to meet this girl.

I decide to give in and say yes. I also volunteer to ask Harry.

This is not as straightforward as it sounds. Harry's bedroom is just down the stairs from mine (our house is very tall and keeps us all fit), but it is a shrine to his music and usually sounds as though it's home to a wild night-club. I have to knock hard.

Harry's practising on his drum kit. When he's not being a photographer, he plays in a band and mixes party playlists for people and occasionally DJs. He's into jazz and retro-funk and French hip-hop. As I said – super-cool. But it's tough getting his attention over MC Solaar and the snare-drum. Eventually, after the fourth bout of knocking, when my knuckles are really starting to hurt, he lets me in.

I tell him about the bazaar and he agrees to bring his camera. Edie'll be pleased.

Then I play my usual game of Svetlana-spotting. Svetlana Russinova is a supermodel and is Harry's latest love – apart from his girlfriend, Moaning Zoe, of course. Harry has a montage of Svetlana pictures above his bed. How Zoe puts up with it, I have no idea. Every time I go into Harry's room I spot new additions to the montage.

Today, Svetlana is advertising a handbag, a perfume and a gold watch. She's also wearing a VERY short dress and high heels for Mario Testino (I'm good at recog-nising photographers – it's a thing I can do). And practically nothing for Rankin.

Zoe, the girlfriend, is short, dark and pierced. She's partial to black leather, and not in a good way. Harry has a very teeny photo of her in an old frame on his bedside table. She's not wearing her glasses and she's squinting a bit.

'What does Zoe think about that one?' I ask, pointing to the Rankin picture of Svetlana, where she's lying on her tummy, doing a crossword, and appears to have given up on getting dressed after putting on some pink silk French knickers.

'She hasn't said,' Harry mutters.

I give him a knowing look. It means, 'I'm no expert, but as far as I know girls don't appreciate their boyfriends admiring other girls' bottoms.'

Harry merely shrugs. 'It's art,' he says.

Yeah right.

I bet Zoe saw it and thought, 'What lovely French knickers. I must get some.' NOT.

Chapter 4

Saturday comes. Jenny is busy being primped and primed, waxed and fake-tanned, squeezed into her new form-fitting super-bra and generally tortured into readiness for her red-carpet moment later on. Harry, Edie and I are on our way to Notting Hill, where Crow's school is holding its bazaar.

We all avoid the seats on the Tube and hang about near the doors. Various people check out my outfit. I dare them to say anything. Nobody does.

'So,' Harry says, giving Edie a friendly smile. 'How's the master plan going? Saved the world yet?'

'Not yet,' she answers, going slightly peach. She's used to being teased by my brother about her plans for world domination, or 'peace', as she calls it.

When she first mentioned the whole United Nations idea, it sounded pretty cool to me.

'Like Angelina Jolie!'

'Angelina Jolie isn't *in* the United Nations,' she told me

wearily. 'She *represents* it sometimes. When she's not acting in movies or adopting people.'

I get the idea Edie isn't as impressed with Angelina Jolie as I am. And I'm not entirely sure what the difference is between being in something and representing it, but whatever it is, Edie wants to do more of it than la Jolie, possibly adopting fewer children in the process.

And whereas Angelina's preparations included acting classes (I'm guessing), Edie's include everything she can think of to impress Harvard University. For example: being top in everything in school, running in the running team, debating with the debating team, playing in the chess club, setting up her own website to promote good causes and volunteering. I think she had some spare time in primary school a few years ago, but I couldn't be sure.

Usually I don't get involved any more. Edie despairs at my superficial life with its 'unhealthy focus' on fashion magazines, customised clothing and celebrity watching. It seems pointless to point out to her that I don't *choose* not to be top in everything and play championship chess; it's something that *happens* to me. And the spare time I have left over from not doing extra maths and orchestra practice (she does that too, I forgot) comes in handy for adapting tee-shirts and leggings and generally trying not to look like every other fourteen-year-old in London.

Today I'm in a floral halter-neck romper suit that I ran up after school one evening. It's supposed to have a sort of thirties tap-dancer vibe. It's cool and comfortable, but

I didn't factor in having to go to the loo, which requires a major planning operation. Harry was very complimentary when I appeared in it this morning. Mum just laughed, but not necessarily in a good way. She'd love Edie's outfit, which is powder blue and pretty and sensible and BORING.

I get a few more strange looks when we arrive at Crow's school. The bazaar is being held on the games pitch, which is an odd description for a large expanse of concrete surrounded by high fencing, but today it's decked out like a village fete, full of bunting and bustling, smiling people. There's a huge banner along one wall of fencing saying 'Welcome to St Christopher's' and dozens of stalls scattered about, selling everything from old books to jewellery and home-made cakes.

Harry immediately whips out his camera and starts snapping away. Edie and I start looking for Crow's stall. I quickly get distracted by some girls selling fabulous neon bangles, then a rather irresistible doughnut stall. I realise it's ages later when Edie tugs on my arm and pulls me along to the far corner of the playground, where the girl in the fairy wings is standing behind the smallest stall in the place.

She's a funny sight. Her head appears much too large for her tiny body. Her face is round and her large lips look made to smile, but they always seem to be pursed in concentration. Her hair is a crazy seventies Afro, on which she has perched two crocheted caps today, side by side.

They look great. Her skin is glistening and gorgeous and spot-free. Jenny would be sooo jealous. From the neck up, she is soul-singer fabulous. From the shoulders down, though, she is like a bony child-bird. Except for her hands, which are beautiful. She has the longest, most graceful fingers I've ever seen.

The stall's a bit of a mess. She has just one table and it's scattered with colourful bits of cheap nylon fabric. She doesn't look up when we get there. She's got her notebook out and she's busy sketching, as usual. If she expects to make a sale, she certainly doesn't show it.

I pick up one of the scraps of fabric.

'How's it going?' Edie asks.

Crow looks up with a scowl. Naomi Campbell on a bad day. She glances at Edie and shrugs. I'm guessing sales haven't been fantastic so far.

'Oi! Fairy.'

A shout comes from behind us. I turn round to see three very pretty blonde sixth-formers in matching minis and open-necked shirts, arranged to show off their flat, tanned, bare midriffs and belly-button piercings. They're all grinning across at Crow. Their stall is selling handbags made out of patchwork squares. Quite nice ones, actually. I feel disloyal for thinking it.

'Got a customer? Ooh, Fairy. Lucky girl! Going to make your fortune?'

They cackle with laughter, amazed at their own cleverness.

'Are they always like that?' asks Edie, indignantly.

Crow shrugs again. Shrugging seems to be her major form of communication. I'm indignant too. I know how it must feel.

'Like the hats, Fairy!' They cackle again. Then one turns to the others and says very loudly, 'D'you remember when she wore that gold cape? Proper little Wonder Woman she was, weren't you, Fairy? Shame it got ruined in that nasty drain.'

They laugh hard, holding on to each other. I can imagine how the cape ended up in the nasty drain. Crow carries on drawing without any change in her expression, though. It's as if they're not there. In fact, she seems to be annoying them far more than they're annoying her.

However, by now Edie and I are more annoyed than anyone.

Edie picks up one of the nylon things.

'How much is it?' she asks.

'Fifty p,' Crow almost whispers, hardly raising her eyes.

'I'll have three,' Edie says loudly. 'Nonie, how about you?'

'Oh, me too,' I agree. 'And one of these.'

There's a raspberry pink knitted thing peeking out from under all the nylon. I'm not sure what it is, but I'm happy to pay two pounds for it.

'And I'll have one as well,' says a voice right behind me. It's Harry. He seems relaxed enough but I can tell from the way he's breathing that he's as annoyed as the rest of us.

Startled, Crow starts putting things in bags and collecting up our proffered coins.

'Actually, we're from *Teen* magazine,' Edie adds after a moment's thought, still keeping her voice up. 'My friend here's our stylist and this is one of our staff photographers. We love your stuff and we'd like to feature you. Such a shame everything else today is so TRASHY. Here's my card.'

She hands something across to Crow, which on inspection turns out to be her library card.

Then she turns on her heel and sweeps off, with me sweeping after her and Harry bringing up the rear, after running off a few shots of the stall for effect.

'Ooooh, Fairy!' we hear just before we head out of earshot. But it sounds like air coming out of a balloon. The blondies' hearts don't seem to be in it any more. And Crow seems to be too busy examining the library card to notice.

Once we're outside the playground, Harry throws his arms around Edie and hugs her.

'Well done! You could be Wonder Woman yourself, you know.' Then he laughs. 'You're shaking.'

She is. I can see it now. It must be a mixture of nerves and indignation.

'We have to DO something,' she splutters.

'I certainly owe her one,' Harry says. 'I got another great picture out of it.'

He scrolls through the pictures on his camera and shows us the one he means. It's of the blondies, all clustered together, looking gorgeous, but positively evil.

'I'm going to call it 'The Three Bitches'. See?'

Edie nods wisely, then sees my dumb expression. 'He means like the three witches. Macbeth. Get it?'

I sigh. It wouldn't surprise me to know she's read all the works of Shakespeare in between the Jane Austens.

'You can have these, by the way,' she adds, thrusting her bag of nylon things at me. 'They're more your style than mine.'

By which she means they're more weird than wonderful, which is probably true. I can't wait to get them home, though, to find out for sure.

Chapter 5

*I*t's late afternoon, and Edie and I are standing in Leicester Square, praying that the unsummery dark-grey clouds that have suddenly appeared don't actually spill their contents onto us until all the people in silk and stilettos have been safely shooed off the red carpet and into the cinema.

Leicester Square is THE place to go for movie pre-mieres. It's got three cinemas and enough places to buy ice cream and hamburgers to keep you going for a year. Normally it's full of pigeons and tourists, but today it's full of red ropes, red carpets, people with walkie-talkies, photographers and us. It's very buzzy and everyone seems to have their mobiles out, hoping to get a picture of a celebrity.

Most of the *Kid Code* stars have arrived and are milling about, posing for photographers and TV cameras. Other famous people and their children keep popping up too, posing quickly and disappearing into the dark of the cinema. They know it would be pointless to try and upstage Hollywood's Hottest Couple, who are happily chatting to people near the ropes and pausing for TV interviews. So is Joe Yule. Briefly, I get a flash from those laser green eyes. I actually go fluttery. Whatever he's got, they should bottle it. I suppose that's sort of what they're doing.

Edie might as well be in double maths, or chess club. She's immune to HHC and even, it appears, to Joe Drool.

'I suspected she was being bullied at school,' she says, 'but now it's obvious. No wonder she hates it so much. This is her fourth school already, you know.'

I can't believe I'm standing in the heart of London's West End, within camera-phone distance of THE TWO MOST FAMOUS PEOPLE IN THE WORLD, and Edie is talking about school bullies. Only Edie.

'What d'you think of my outfit, by the way?' I ask.

She looks at me appraisingly. 'Bizarre, obviously. But not bad. It suits you.'

'It's Crow's stuff.'

'No!'

It turns out that the strange nylon things were skirts. They look like nothing at all when they're folded up, but as soon as you put them on they puff and billow into beautiful shapes. Each one is different. I've tried all six of them on, and tonight I've gone for the violet one with points shaped like inverted tulip petals. I'm also wearing the knitted thing I bought, which looked like a lump in the bag but morphed into the warmest, lightest jumper. It's like wearing a cobweb crossed with an Arctic jacket. Perfect for this cloudy weather. And it's somehow managed to give me hips, which (like cheekbones) I absolutely don't possess in real life.

More famous people troop across the red carpet. Edie spots a junior Cabinet Minister. I spot two Sugarbabes. Then, finally, yet another car with darkened windows pulls up and a familiar pair of knees emerges from the back door.

'Here she is!' I squeal. Even Edie has the decency to squeal too.

Gradually the knees give way to a glimpse of thigh and the bottom of the cherry tomato. Cameras flash. Holding firmly to the hem of her dress, Jenny inches nervously along the rest of the seat and manoeuvres herself out of the car. I can see why finishing schools have classes in this sort of thing.

She stands beside the car, waiting, while a fat old man in a dinner jacket squeezes out beside her. We scream to grab her attention, but everyone else is screaming too, so she doesn't hear us. Her hair has been curled into tight ringlets. Someone has decided it would be a good idea to give her lots of shiny green eye-makeup. And whoever did the fake tan got more than slightly carried away. She is orange from the hemline down.

Not so much a cherry tomato any more. More of a traffic light.

Jenny smiles nervously into the bank of flashing cameras. Fat bloke beside her (her father) takes her by the elbow and some men in black suits with walkie-talkies guide them both towards the red carpet. From the look on her face, it might as well be the guillotine.

Once she's there, Hollywood's Hottest Female gives her a brief wave of acknowledgement. Her husband flashes a smile. Joe Yule, on the other hand, is suddenly busy signing things for a group of fans and talking into their phones.

Jenny's dad works hard, on the lookout for TV presenters to talk to and grinning madly at anyone with a camera, including the crowd. For a while, Jenny wafts around vaguely in his wake. Finally, she spots our frantic waving and gives us a bit of a smile. It's hard to tell from this distance, but I would swear she looks almost tearful. Then suddenly the men with walkie-talkies are closing in and she's ushered through the doors and into the cinema. It's all over.

'How d'you think she looked?' Edie asks. This is, after all, my area of expertise.

I try for a few seconds, screwing up my face with the effort, but nothing will come.

When your best friend has just been standing outside the biggest cinema in Leicester Square, near one of the sexiest women in the world who happens to be dressed in form-fitting Armani Privé, sky-high Manolos and matching husband, and your friend looks like a traffic light, standing next to a fat, baggy guy with fake hair, there is no fashion vocabulary that can adequately capture the moment.

Chapter 6

The next day, I'm trying to catch up on some French grammar in the garden when I get a text: 'In Drchster 1/2 hr off, pls cm nw. HELP!!!!!!'

Jenny's doing her promotional tour. She's installed in the poshest hotel on Park Lane, faced with a stream of journalists who've seen the film and want to talk to her about it. She gave me her list of instructions for managing their questions:

Don't talk about Hollywood's Hottest Couple, except as actors.

Don't talk about Joe Yule's girlfriend (rumours they are splitting up).

Don't talk about that incident with the peanut butter, the honey and the fire extinguisher in Egypt.

Make sure the film poster can be seen behind you at all times.

Tell the funny story about the monkey when you were on location in Morocco.

Don't say what Hollywood's Hottest Female said to the monkey.

And so on for pages and pages. She's already told the monkey story about fifty thousand times. And she didn't find it funny the first time. And every journalist's first question is always about Joe Yule's girlfriend, so she has to start every interview saying she can't comment, which she hates. I can imagine that she needs a quick shoulder to cry on, so I shove one of Crow's skirts over my romper suit (I'm not sure if the Dorchester allows romper suits) and tell Mum where I'm going. Ten minutes later, I'm there.

Edie's obviously had a text too. We meet at reception. Edie's in a grey printed summer dress that covers her knees and matching ballet slippers. I doubt she needed to change. She was probably wearing it to do her homework.

'She's on her way down,' says a tall bloke behind the desk. 'You might like to go outside.' He's looking at my legs. It turns out the petal skirt is transparent in daylight and I might as well not have bothered.

But outside is fine. As soon as Jenny sees us she flings her arms around us and takes us across the road to Hyde Park, where the sun is shining, the grass is endless and the romper suit seems totally appropriate.

Then she promptly bursts into floods of tears.

She's clutching some folded sheets of paper. Edie takes them from her and spreads them out. They're from one of the Sunday papers. On the front page are two pictures: one of Hollywood's Hottest Couple looking gorgeous in Armani from last night, and another of Jenny half-hiding behind her dad, looking traffic-light-ish. The headline says 'Exclusive! Theatre Knight's Happy Ending'. Inside is the article. As Jenny sobs on, Edie reads out the opening paragraph.

'Last night, Sir Lionel Merritt was proudly accompanying his daughter Jenny on the red carpet at the premiere of the new blockbuster, Kid Code. *As the cameras flashed and the stars posed, few people could imagine the great man's recent heartache, and the happiness he has finally found with the woman who rekindled the flame in theatre's enfant terrible.'*

It turns out that Sir Lionel has decided that now's the time to leave his third wife for his latest mistress, and Jenny's premiere is the ideal way of getting the publicity to finance the divorce and the 'exquisite Cotswolds home' he's setting up with wife-to-be number four. There's an awful lot about Sir Lionel and his various stage productions thirty years ago, but newspapers need family appeal, so he's padded it out with the few bits of Jenny's childhood he was around for, her mother's 'tragic' nervous breakdown (which coincidentally happened around the time he left her for wife three), and Jenny's embarrassment about her boobs, spots and weight. He rounds it off by wishing her well and promising he'll always stick by her, as 'theatre is in the Merritt blood'.

Edie finishes the article with a look of disbelief.

'That man is evil!'

'He's just . . . Dad, I guess,' Jenny mumbles. She's at the hiccupping stage now. 'He needed the money. The funny thing is, he invited me to that house in the Cotswolds last night. He said if I wanted to spend the summer there, I could. It sounded quite nice. Mum wants to murder him, of course.'

I look back down at the paper.

'Has anybody mentioned it?' I ask. 'Today, I mean. In there.' I indicate the Dorchester, across the road.

Jenny looks at me as though I've gone barmy.

'*Mentioned* it? I was all ready with the lousy monkey story. I was geared up to talk about Joe Yule's incredible talent till I was blue in the face. And all they've asked me all morning, for the last four hours, is "What's it like growing boobs when you're in the public eye?" "What do you use for your spots?" "Have you got any messages for fat teenage girls?" "What's it like growing up with a famous father?" And I don't even know, 'cause he was never there.'

I look at her, hunched up on the grass, makeup streaming. (She doesn't normally wear it, but they slap it on thick for those TV interviews.) She's in her usual jeans and some black cotton top they've given her, which billows over the boobs while suggesting that underneath its capacious covering they may be the size of hot-air balloons. A large, fierce spot has emerged on her cheek since last night and is sitting there defiantly, soaking up the midday sun.

'Anyway,' she says, desperate to change the subject, 'what did you think of yesterday?'

There's a long pause while I will Edie not to mention the traffic-light effect. Luckily, she's distracted before she can say anything. A bus is heading down Park Lane with a picture of Jenny's face on it, two metres high, beside Joe Yule's. She looks spotless. Literally. And supermodel thin. It's kind of surreal to see her this way. Especially as real, runny-makeup Jenny is sitting beside us. Edie bobs up and down and points. We look over.

'They airbrushed me!' Jenny says, affronted. 'They even airbrushed my neck! I would've said that was the one bit of me that wasn't spotty or podgy, but they had to airbrush that.'

Edie and I exchange despairing looks. Our cheering-up job isn't going as well as I'd hoped. I absent-mindedly play with the petals of my new skirt while I try to think of something positive to say.

'That's unusual,' Jenny says at last, looking at the skirt. 'Did you make it?'

Relieved at the chance not to talk about *Kid Code* or Sir Lionel Merritt for a moment, we tell her all about the bazaar. Edie explains about the Three Bitches. I butt in with Edie's super-amazing rescue mission and the library card. We both interrupt each other. Jenny's eyes swing between us as if she's watching a tennis match. By the time we've finished, her eyes have dried and her streaky face is smiling.

'If only you *had* been from *Teen* magazine.'

We all look a bit helpless for a minute. We are so NOT from *Teen* magazine. If it exists, even.

'Those girls have to be stopped, though. I'm going to complain to the people I volunteer with,' Edie says crossly. 'There must be something they can do.'

'I think her main problem was the nylon,' I add.

Edie and Jenny both look at me as though I've completely lost it.

'How can I help?' Jenny asks Edie. She's obviously given up on me as a lost cause.

This is tricky. Jenny's going to be out of the country for the next few weeks.

'Maybe you could email her descriptions of what people are wearing in New York and Tokyo?' I suggest. 'To give her ideas for making stuff.'

Edie maintains her pitying look.

'She can hardly read and she hasn't got a computer. Apart from that, brilliant.'

I'm crushed.

'Maybe you could bring her back stuff, then,' I mumble.

'It'll do as a start,' Jenny says. Then she suddenly realises that she's overrun her break time and is hopelessly late.

'I'm in such big trouble!' she wails dramatically, then

giggles. 'What can they do to me, though? Edit me out of the film?'

We accompany her back to the hotel's reception, where FOUR PR people are standing in their black suits, on various phones and BlackBerries, looking out nervously for her. It's like being met by four angry parents after a late evening out. Much as we love her, we leave her to it. She doesn't seem to mind too much. She's used to it by now.

It's only later, back in the sunshine, that I realise I forgot to ask her about Joe Yule. Something strange was happening on that red carpet yesterday. Was he deliberately avoiding her? Too late now. I know she won't trust anything sensitive to texts or emails while she's away – she's been warned about them being intercepted. Honestly, knowing a couple of Hollywood stars is like joining the CIA. So it may be a while until I finally wheedle the truth out of her.

Chapter 7

$\mathcal{I}$t's near the end of summer term, so exams are over, classes are winding down and homework is minimal. This gives Edie plenty of time to think about the Three Bitches.

'I've told the special needs people,' she informs me one day in maths. 'But I'm not convinced they can do very much. The one thing they did say was that Crow needs more friends. I'd have thought that was obvious. They suggested I should try and befriend her more. I've tried, but we don't really have much in common.'

She gives me a look and the light comes on in that superbrain of hers. For once, I'm right there with her.

'Invite her over,' I say. 'She can come any time.'

And so she comes.

She looks at my wall of *Vogue* photo shoots and my other wall of costume exhibition posters from the V&A, and I can tell she's in heaven.

She snuggles herself into my favourite armchair, the purple velvet one, and tells us about her sketches and V&A visits and making clothes after school. It turns out she's on her own a lot, so she goes off to look at clothes, or she just invents them at home with whatever fabrics she can find. And she's always drawing her ideas. Pages and pages and pages of them.

I ask about her family, but she looks past me and I wonder if she's heard me. Then she says something about growing up in Uganda, where her parents and several of her aunts and uncles and cousins are, and leaving them to come to England when she was eight.

'Why?' I ask, appalled. I mean, I love England, but leaving your family to come here seems a bit extreme.

Crow looks at the floor and shrugs. For ages, she says nothing, but we wait. Eventually she looks up.

'It was difficult in my country. My dad wanted me to get an English education. When my little sister is older, maybe she'll come too.'

'How often do you see your parents?' I wonder. My dad lives in Paris. Mum met him when she was modelling there. I see him twice a year, which really isn't enough at all. Harry's dad is in Brazil (Mum travelled a lot), which is worse.

'Not so much.'

'How much?'

'Never,' she almost whispers. 'They send photos. My sister Victoria sends me her drawings. She's four now.

Nearly five.' She reaches into her satchel and pulls out some folded sheets of paper. They are covered in pictures of smiling children with stick fingers and triangular, colourful clothes under bright blue skies. They are confidently signed 'Victoria' in careful four-year-old writing.

'So who do you live with?'

'My Auntie Florence. She came here years ago. She cleans at my school. She works very hard.'

Edie and I both smile encouragingly. We're not sure what to say.

On Crow's second visit, my room is a tip. I've had an idea for a mini-dress and I've been raiding my bookshelves for inspiration. The books are everywhere and there are lots of them. I'm not exactly literary, but if it's a book about fashion, I have to have it. Mum, Dad and Granny are very generous (although Dad does insist on giving them to me in French, so I can practise). I have everything from serious histories of couture to cut-out paper dolls. I've been collecting them since I was seven. Most of them are lying open on the carpet and I desperately try and clear a path so Crow can get across the room without treading on them.

However, she doesn't move. She's spellbound. Edie gives me an astonished stare. She's never seen Crow look enthusiastic about a book before.

The great thing about fashion books, of course, is the illustrations. Huge, full-page photographs and beautiful drawings. Crow's eye darts from a Balenciaga ballgown to an Elizabethan ruff. She crouches down and runs her fingers over the pages.

'Does this say Dior?' she asks.

'Yes,' Edie says, instantly switching into teacher mode. 'And that says Christian. His . . . er . . . Christian name.'

'Dior is my hero,' Crow breathes. 'There's this woman called Yvette who lives upstairs. She worked for Dior. She's teaching me to knit and sew. She tells me all about him.'

Edie and I exchange glances. We both suspect that someone is taking advantage of this innocent little girl from Africa with romantic, unlikely stories. After all, Christian Dior died fifty years ago.

'May I take it?'

She's indicating the fattest book in the pile. It's a history of the House of Dior and it's written like a text-book. It's not exactly the Famous Five.

'Certainly,' says Edie, looking shocked. 'I mean, she can, can't she, Nonie?'

'Of course,' I shrug. 'Take whatever you like.'

To our amazement, Crow chooses five books and happily piles them up. It occurs to me that maybe she'd have learnt to read long ago if people had started her off with cocktail dresses and ballgowns, instead of kittens and puppies.

Edie texts me after her next volunteering session to say they've already finished page one. Which, for someone who struggles with 'chair' isn't bad going, I think.

Something's still bothering me, though.

I'm convinced those skirts and knits we got from the bazaar are amazing, but nobody really believes me. It's not helped by the fact that I have a reputation for wearing anything, including Astroturf (which looks great as a miniskirt, by the way, although it's a bit scratchy when you sit down). I think the biggest problem is that Crow's designs are made out of cheap fabrics in gaudy colours, which is all that she can afford. But I have a plan.

I interrupt Harry in the middle of another drumming practice.

'Harry, you know Moaning Zoe . . .'

'I wish you wouldn't refer to my girlfriend as Moaning Zoe. Especially not to her face. She doesn't like it.'

'I bet she moans about it.'

'Actually, she does. But, I think that's totally justified.'

'Well, does she have any friends?'

'Nonie!'

'What?'

'Please do not suggest that my girlfriend is sad and friendless.'

'Sorry, didn't mean to. I was just wondering if she knew anyone who made things out of ordinary stuff. Like cotton. Or even silk.'

Moaning Zoe is in her final year at St Martins. She's doing textiles. In Zoe's case, 'textiles' is a loose description because she mostly makes things out of cardboard, as far as I can tell. Or circuit boards. Or old mobile phone covers. All very trendy and eco-friendly, but not exactly what I have in mind. She makes Astroturf look positively normal.

'Zoe is very talented,' Harry sniffs. 'In her own way. But she's got friends who do more conventional things. There's a girl called Skye who's nice. She sings with the band sometimes. Why?'

I explain my theory about providing Crow with better materials but that I have no idea how to get hold of them for her in large quantities. I'm convinced that a textiles student would know. Presumably they cover that sort of thing in week one.

And so the following Saturday – the day Jenny's leaving for New York – Skye comes over. Girls tend to do things if Harry asks them. I like her immediately. She has orange hair with shocking pink streaks and is wearing a floor-length dress made out of tie-dyed parachute silk and Doc Marten boots. No makeup and a constant smile. She's a walking ray of sunshine.

Crow's already ensconced in my room, on page three of the House of Dior book, running her finger carefully along each line. She looks up when we come in and gives a shy smile. Today she's wearing her Wonder Woman cape (rescued from the drain) and a home-made Elizabethan ruff. It's a look. We all cluster round a pile of multicoloured nylon and I do a bit of a fashion show, whipping the skirts on and off over my leggings and showing how beautifully they move when I walk.

Skye is impressed. She instantly gets what I mean about using silk and offers Crow all the offcuts she doesn't need. She explains that she's finalising her degree show at the moment, so she's got loads of spare fabric, and she happens to be working with painted silk, among other things.

Her face clouds for a moment.

'This silk's incredibly difficult to work with. I've tried it myself. It's super-slippery. Are you sure you can manage?'

Crow looks relaxed.

'Yvette – she's the woman who's teaching me to sew – she used to work for Dior. She specialised in silk. She's shown me all the techniques.'

Skye throws me a questioning look and I shrug. Best to humour her, we silently agree. Anyway, somebody must be teaching Crow to sew because the skirts are beautifully made and very cleverly cut. Skye says they wouldn't look out of place in a St Martins show. I'm amazed, but Crow doesn't seem particularly impressed. However, she's excited about getting her hands on new fabrics. It turns out she's got a notebook full of designs she's been dying to try, but she simply can't afford the materials to make them.

'Are you sure that girl is twelve?' Skye asks on the way out.

It's weird. Crow looks about ten, and behaves like a ten-year-old in some ways. She can be very stubborn, for a start, and she just ignores you if she doesn't want to answer a question. But as soon as you start to talk about fashion, you'd swear she was at least twenty. And because we talk about fashion most of the time, I tend to forget.

Mind you, I'm only fourteen and I'd swear I was twenty sometimes. And Edie must be at least fifty in her head.

In the evening, Harry's phone goes at supper. It's a text from Moaning Zoe. He starts reading it with his normal, gentle expression, but soon his smile fades and he looks, for Harry, pretty grumpy.

'Is she OK?' I ask.

'She's heard from a friend that Skye was here. She wants to know why.'

'Goodness! News travels fast.'

'I'm not sure I like being spied on,' Harry says, passing a hand distractedly through his hair.

'But she'll be OK when you explain,' I suggest.

'Yeah, probably.'

That's what he says, but he doesn't look too sure.

Chapter 8

*N*ext day, Harry agrees to come with Edie and me to the cinema to see *Kid Code*, which Jenny would only let us do when she was safely out of the country. We invite Crow, but she's already had her first consignment of silk from Skye and she's too busy inspecting it and working out what to do with it. No sign of Moaning Zoe. Harry says she's busy preparing for her own degree show, but you have to wonder.

Kid Code is as good as the critics say. With that cast the producers could have got away with a tired old formula blockbuster, but actually it's really funny and so exciting Edie nearly chokes on her popcorn at one point. No wonder the audiences are pouring in. Hollywood's Hottest Couple give the best performances we've seen them do, and Joe Yule is POSITIVELY EDIBLE.

The only dodgy bits are when he's with his rather wooden sister. Poor Jenny. You can see the sheer terror in her eyes whenever the camera is on her. Even Joe's

English accent seems better than hers after a while, and he's from Nevada.

And, golly, those eyes of his. I have a feeling I may need to see the film again soon, to appreciate the full depth of his performance – obviously.

Over the last few days, the glossy celebrity magazines have been hitting the shelves with full-page spreads about the London premiere. I buy every one. They all agree that the movie is good, but their real focus is on the red carpet and what everyone is wearing. HHC, in their matching Armani, are sparkling. Every possible opportunity is taken to ogle them from every angle. Joe Yule, playing it cool in his Zac Posen jacket and tie to match his eyes, is perfect in every way.

Jenny features heavily too. Most magazines have found space for an article about her father, the multiple wives and news of Jenny's struggle with spots and boobs. Each one is illustrated with the cherry tomato. Somehow the pictures and the articles seem to suit each other perfectly, as if she had deliberately chosen the dress to highlight the plight of the chubby, miserable teenager. She makes it into the 'hit and miss' pages too, where she is an outright car crash in every one. And this week she's up against a pregnant glamour girl in head-to-toe leopard skin and a pop star in a yellow Lurex micro-mini and Uggs.

It's different when it's someone you know on those pages. I feel so guilty buying the magazines, but sadly it doesn't stop me. The images seem to be everywhere. Even Mum, who normally sticks to *Vogue* and *Art Monthly*, notices. She doesn't usually pay much attention to my friends, but she likes Jenny. She saw her in *Annie* at school and thought she was incredible.

'What that girl needs,' Mum says, 'is corsetry.'

What that girl needs, I think, is therapy.

The New York premiere of *Kid Code* is shown live on an entertainment channel on cable. I have to stay up late to catch it, accompanied by Harry (still no Zoe), Phish Food ice cream and Maryland cookies. (It drives Jenny potty that I can eat anything and always remain extremely skinny, but my metabolism is the one useful thing I've inherited from Mum.)

The presenters are already raving about the movie, which promises to be as popular in New York as in London. Hollywood's Hottest Couple are looking chic in yet more Armani. They must have some kind of deal going. Joe Yule is achingly gorgeous, as ever. He's got Sexy Girlfriend with him this time and she's clinging to him like a limpet, wearing the smallest micro-dress I've ever seen to show off her perfect legs.

Jenny's legs, on the other hand, are nowhere to be seen. Pablo Dodo has decided that this time she is best served by a bubblegum pink maxi-dress that skims her ankles after bulging around her boobs and hips. This is accessorised with flat sandals and a floaty boa thing that she's hugging to herself like a life jacket.

Joe Yule is ignoring her again. Jenny's father, not surprisingly, is banned. HHC are so busy being mobbed by journalists and photographers they don't have time for her. She stands there alone, clutching her boa thing in the flashing lights, panicking.

I glance across at Harry, who's watching her through his fingers, as if he can hardly bear to look.

No need to ask him what he thinks. And I decide not to share my thoughts, either. Because she reminds me of nothing so much as a giant, pink, miserable condom. In a boa.

Chapter 9

'*D*on't *ever* tell her I told you that,' I say menacingly.
    'I won't, promise!' Edie splutters. Her voice is
muffled by a bunch of purple and green things in cello-
phane.

I'm deeply regretting sharing the condom image with
Edie. We were messaging each other and I was trying to
give the full impact of the sheer awfulness of the maxi-
dress disaster. For an instant, I forgot that Edie's cleverness and her reliability with embarrassing information
are at opposite ends of the scale.

But it's too late now, and anyway, we're busy. We're in
a grubby building just off Gloucester Road, standing on
the staircase that leads up to Crow's flat. Her Auntie
Florence wants to meet us.

The smell is the thing I notice most of all. I think
something must have died in the flat downstairs. Possibly
a mouse. Or maybe a family of them.

'Perhaps on cold days it's not so bad,' says Edie

hopefully. She's lucky. She's holding the bunch of flowers we've bought with us and she can shove her face in them, like an Elizabethan lady with a nosegay.

Crow says the invitation is to say thank you for the reading stuff and helping her out with the new fabrics. Edie suspects it's to make sure we're not a couple of slave-traders or child-molesters and I think she's probably right. So I've borrowed one of Edie's skirts and a top-thing to look respectable. The skirt is hanging off me and the top-thing is straining over even my modest boobage, so they're not having quite the effect I was after. I look more like a wild gypsy princess than a budding royal. Edie, as usual, looks as though she's dressed for tea at the British Embassy.

The door opens and a tall, elegant but exhausted-looking woman lets us in. Edie offers her the flowers and she thanks us with a smile. I'm guessing she doesn't get them on a regular basis.

'I'm Florence,' she says. 'Pleased to meet you.' We shake her hand.

Inside there is a main room with a couple of doors leading off it. The kitchen is in one corner. Another corner has a low table and a couple of chairs and a stool, where we are motioned to sit.

'Elizabeth!' the woman calls loudly, as if the sound might have to carry down a couple of corridors. A door opens about half a metre away and Crow appears. Apparently, Crow is Elizabeth. Confusing. Behind her, I can see a tiny room, hardly bigger than the bed, hung from floor to ceiling with knitwear and dresses in various stages of design. How Crow can even breathe among that lot, I can't imagine.

She comes through obediently and helps her aunt bring a couple of paper plates from the kitchen area. We're treated to crisps and biscuits and cups of super-strong tea. I notice the lack of anything on the walls. Coming from a home that is practically an art gallery, I find this physically painful. There are just two photographs in little wooden frames. One is of a tall, elegant man who looks like the male version of Florence, with a woman and a little girl – Crow's family, I assume. The other is a school picture of Crow, looking sullen and watchful and under-accessorised.

Florence explains how grateful she is to us for providing some company for her niece. She doesn't seem to be worried about the slave trade thing at all.

'I have two jobs. I work every day, unless I'm sick. I'm hardly ever here to talk to Elizabeth. She's a hard worker too. Every day she's always making something. She has Yvette' – the woman 'from Dior' – 'but she's an old, old lady. Crow needs people her own age. She needs children.'

We smile respectfully. Fourteen-year-olds love being categorised as children. Yes indeedy. Totally with the programme.

Edie picks up the photograph of the man, the woman and the little girl.

'Your brother?' she asks.

'Yes. James. He's a teacher. A very responsible man. He's passionate about England and anything English, isn't he, Elizabeth?'

Crow nods. I'm struggling with the Elizabeth–Crow thing. It's a strange nickname and not linked to her real name at all. Edie says she's asked and Crow won't talk about it. Clams up like Harrison Ford in an interview (Edie didn't say that of course, but that's the impression I get). Odd.

'His little girl is Victoria,' Florence continues. 'English queens, you see? He's so proud that Elizabeth is here, getting a proper, English education.'

I spot Edie flinch. She's talked to Crow about this and she knows the education is not exactly perfect when there are thirty of you in the class and you can't read ninety per cent of what the teacher writes or anything in your textbook. Crow mostly just sits at her desk and doodles on her notebooks, praying she won't be asked a question. She likes art, though.

'Will James come to England too?' Edie asks.

'Oh, no. He teaches in a camp for displaced people. He can't leave them. And Grace can't leave him, and little Victoria can't leave Grace.'

'Why . . . ?' I don't know how to put it exactly, without being rude. I struggle. I just don't understand how it could possibly be better for Crow to be in this tiny flat, with an aunt who's never there, instead of at home, with her family. It seems such an important question it's almost too obvious to ask. And yet I can't find the words to phrase it.

Edie notices me struggling and puts a hand on my arm. For once, she gives me the look I've so often had to give her: the 'don't go there' look. I'm still desperate to find out more, but when I give the look to Edie, I seriously mean 'shut up,' so I take a dose of my own medicine and ask instead about how Crow's getting on with all her new materials.

This is obviously the right decision. Crow leaps up delightedly and takes me into her room to show me. We leave Edie and Florence to talk.

I don't know what to take in first. There's the size of the room – tiny; the furniture – a few bits of old office stuff, including a filing cabinet; the walls – covered in fabulous illustrations of dancing girls, pictures by Victoria and torn-out pages from magazines; and the sculpture-skirts and dresses – everywhere.

Crow must be obsessed. They're piled several layers deep. Paper patterns. Practice versions in cheap cotton. Violent-coloured nylon examples and now delicate silk versions that look like melted works of art. They're hanging from the curtain rail. Hanging from the handles of the filing cabinet. Draped on the bed. Folded on and under the tiny desk, where the only object I can recognise between the piles is an old, black, hand-operated Singer sewing machine.

'How long have you been making these?' I ask.

'Two years,' Crow says. 'Before, I just knitted. It was so cold when I came to London. But then I went to the V&A with Yvette. I saw Balenciaga. Vionnet. Now I practise.'

Good grief. I usually think that removing a collar or slapping on a few sequins (or Tipp-Ex) is pretty creative. Next to this kid I'm obviously hopeless and destined not even to be allowed to make the tea for a designer. I find a small spot on the floor to sit down, lost in wonder and sad contemplation of my future career at McDonalds.

I have an idea, though. There may be one other thing I can do to help.

'Can I borrow a couple of things?' I ask. 'I promise I'll bring them back.'

Crow gives a shrug that I interpret as a yes. I take one of the new silk skirts and a couple of Crow's sketches that are lying in an untidy pile near the sewing machine. Needless to say, they're brilliant. Bright, spiky dancing girls cavorting round the pages in light-as-air dresses and vertiginous heels. The kind of thing I've been trying to draw since I was six. Crow doesn't ask what they're for, but although she thinks I'm slightly barmy, she does seem to trust me, which is encouraging.

As we leave the room, Edie and Florence hurriedly wind up their conversation. Both of them are mopping their eyes.

'Thank you,' Florence says, wrapping me in a bear hug with her strong frame. She does the same for Edie.

'That girl's a genius,' I tell her. 'Seriously.'

Florence smiles thinly. 'Her school says she needs extra help. She's special needs.'

'She's special all right.'

Now it's Florence's turn to shrug. We leave them in the tiny flat and make our way back past the smell of dead mouse. Three streets away, all the houses are owned by millionaires. London is crazy.

Chapter 10

'So?'

Edie looks innocent. 'So?'

'So what did Florence say?'

We're back in Edie's room and it's late. Her little brother Jake went to bed hours ago. I'm sleeping over and her mum has just informed us that 'sleep means sleep,' but we have far too much to talk about. We weren't really in the mood on the way back from our visit, but now I feel ready to catch up and Edie is busy on Google and Wikipedia, looking up the missing facts in the story she got from Florence.

'She said what I suspected,' Edie says, with more than a hint of smugness.

'Which was?'

'Well, I tried to talk to you about it before, last week, but you said it was dull and distasteful.'

'I think I was trying to watch *Gossip Girl* at the time,' I point out.

'Obviously you had better things to do.'

'It was a major episode. Anyway. Tell me now.'

Edie hesitates. I can tell part of her doesn't want to, because I wasn't listening the first time. But another part simply loves explaining things to people who don't know stuff, and this is the part that wins.

'Well,' she begins, 'lots of Uganda is perfectly safe and normal. The Queen's been there. But Crow comes from the north, near Sudan, and things are different there. The Government's been fighting a rebel group called the Lord's Resistance Army for years and years. The rebels hide out in the bush and use children to fight. When things were really bad, they used to kidnap boys from their homes at night and make them maim and kill people. Even their own families. The girls were made to have the soldiers' babies. So children who lived in remote villages used to walk miles and miles every afternoon to somewhere safe in a town, where there were people to protect them. They did it night after night, sleeping where they could. They were called night walkers.'

'And Crow was one?'

'Yes. That's why her parents sent her here as soon as they could. Florence doesn't like to talk about it in front of Crow. The memories, you know . . .'

'But now? You said things *were* really bad. Are they better?'

Edie frowns. 'Not completely. They're having peace talks, but the rebels still haven't given in. I've been checking. Look.' She turns her head back to her screen. 'Thousands of people are still too scared to return to their villages. Or they don't have villages to return to. They're living in camps in tiny huts all packed together, in fear of bandits. And James and Grace, Crow's parents, are trying to help them. James is one of the few qualified teachers. He's trying to help the children learn something, even without books and desks and blackboards. But he's in danger too. So Crow can't go back. You see? Or she could, but from where he's sitting how could a life in Kensington possibly be worse than a life in a camp? As far as he's concerned, she's one of the lucky ones. If things don't get better, he'll send Victoria when she's old enough.'

It's hard to imagine. I mean, I know this sort of thing is always happening somewhere in the world, but it's hard to imagine it affecting people I know. It's hard to picture that tall, elegant man in the photograph deciding to send his daughters to a country where he can't see them grow up. It's hard to think of Crow packing up her things every afternoon and walking for miles, with only other children for company. In London, you'd probably be arrested. And it's impossible to imagine what would have happened if the rebels had got her. It is for me, anyway. Edie seems to have imagined it all.

'What are you doing now?'

Edie's rattling away at her computer, her fingers flying over the keys.

'I'm setting up some new links on my website. You know I've got all that stuff about recycling and fresh water for villages?'

'Yes.'

'Well, I'm going to add some pages about Invisible Children. Those are all the ones who've been displaced by this war. Boys and girls with no proper homes, no proper education. Lots of them have been split up from their families. There's this campaign to help them. I'd never heard about it before. And *I'm* actually interested in this stuff. So it obviously needs lots more publicity.'

'Edie, I hate to say this, but how many people look at your website?'

'About two thousand a week.'

'Oh? Really?'

Edie rarely mentions her website. She's been running it for a year now, between homework, chess, orchestra and the other stuff. As it's about water and recycling, it's not exactly YouTube for entertainment value. I was expecting her to say she gets about four visitors and I was going to explain, kindly, that putting links on her website wasn't really going to make a huge amount of difference. But two thousand sounds quite impressive.

'Yes, really. They like my blog, mostly. I talk about what I'm up to. What you're wearing, obviously. School stuff. And what I really care about and what I think we should do about it. I get loads of comments and questions. Lots of other bloggers point to me now. Look.'

We spend the next half hour skipping backwards and forwards across links in the internet, revealing a network of Edies across Europe and America and Africa, all trying to change the world and talking to each other about it. I had no idea. I'm quite glad to realise she's not alone, because obviously she doesn't get a huge amount of sense out of me on most of these subjects. Just as I find her a bit limited on the history of punk or the advisability of the gladiator sandal.

'Hang on a minute!' It's just sunk in. 'Do you tell two thousand people a week what I'm *wearing*?'

'Yes,' Edie says, as if it's the most natural thing in the world. 'You don't mind, do you? Some of them are quite interested.'

Chapter 11

I wake up next morning and my brain is aching.

First, there's the thought that the little girl who likes to wear fairy wings was nearly captured by rebels and made into a soldier or a slave. And the worst thing that's ever happened to me was forgetting to wear knickers to games when I was nine. (Actually, that was pretty bad, but I still don't think it's up there against the whole rebel army scenario.)

Second, there's the memory of all those incredible outfits that Crow's been busy designing for the last couple of years. All tucked away in that tiny, overcrowded box room.

Third, there's the picture that Jenny's just texted me of herself at the LA premiere of *Kid Code*. They put her in a YELLOW TROUSER SUIT. No words come. Things can't possibly get any worse. What have they got in mind for her in Tokyo? A gold bikini?

Fourth, and worst, I have to think of something clever

to wear this afternoon, because I'm about to be surrounded by some of the coolest dressers on the planet
and I now know that Edie is going to describe me to
TWO THOUSAND STRANGERS ON THE INTERNET.
Which is pretty freaky.

It's Moaning Zoe's degree show at St Martins. Harry's
invited me for company and sweetly, Skye – who's also
graduating – has invited Crow. I'm in no fit mental state
to go, but I have to, to support Harry. Something bad is
going on with Moaning Zoe and he may need my help.
First, though: what to wear.

It takes two hours and my bed starts to look like something out of 'The Princess and the Pea' under all the
discarded ideas. Eventually, I opt for my Converses, black
sequinned leggings, a white school shirt (which is fine as
long as you NEVER wear a white shirt to school, obviously), Mum's Galliano waistcoat that I'm not allowed to
borrow on PAIN OF DEATH and a necklace I've made
out of Haribos. Edible art. Perfect if things get really
stressful.

Harry goes for jeans, a loose linen shirt with several
rips in it and flip-flops, and looks great, if somewhat
casual.

Things don't start well.

It takes a while to find Zoe. Eventually I spot her in a
dark corner of a room lit by colourful but not very effec-
tive neon tubes. She's snogging a boy in a tailored jacket,

chains and leather jeans. I watch in disgust, waiting for one of them to look up, but they don't. They just keep at it. Eventually, they reach Discovery Channel proportions of snoggery and I am simply fascinated. How do they breathe, for example? How do they get their noses to fit so close together? And how do they manage not to get their facial piercings caught on each other?

After what seems like hours, Harry comes over and stands beside me, thoughtfully.

'I think she's trying to tell you something,' I say.

'I'd noticed.'

'Anyone you know?'

'Her name's Zoe. She used to be my girlfriend.'

I giggle. 'No, I meant him.'

'His name's Sven and he's Svedish. Look, this is his stuff over here.'

Harry leads me over to a display of what looks like fisherman's netting, complete with fish, seaweed and abandoned bits of rubbish.

'It's supposed to be a searing comment on global pollution. Particularly of the high seas. Maybe Sven's ancestors were Vikings.'

'And people are supposed to make clothes out of it? I can't exactly see Ralph Lauren going for it. Or Prada.'

'I think Sven's a conceptual artist, really,' Harry muses. 'He'll be fine with Zoe.'

We look across at Zoe's masterpieces, which are lined up nearby. They appear to be made out of melted and stretched water bottles, complete with their old labels. In addition to looking highly uncomfortable and sweat-inducing, they are also see-through. I've never been convinced by Zoe as a designer and from what I've seen this evening I guess Harry was more attracted by her snogging skills. But he doesn't seem too distraught that he won't be on the receiving end of them any more.

Zoe breaks for air and looks across at us.

'Oh, hi Harry,' she says, as if she's just noticed him. 'Hi . . .'

She and Harry have been going out for five months, which is not long enough for her to have registered my name. Sven lowers his mouth back onto hers for more resuscitation. Harry gives them a friendly wave.

'Are you OK?' I ask, reaching up to put a sisterly arm around his waist.

Harry nods convincingly.

'She was a bit clingy. Like some of her textiles. And besides, I'm in love.'

I goggle. This is superfast.

'Who? Not Skye?'

He gives me his pitying look.

'No-ooo,' he says, as if addressing a very small, stupid child. 'Her picture's all over my room, dummy.'

'Oh, not Svetlana!'

'And why not?'

'Hmm. Let me think. Two reasons. She's a SUPER-MODEL. And her father's a Russian BILLIONAIRE.'

'And your point is?'

My brother can be very dim sometimes.

'Well, Harry, you're lovely and everything and you're my brother and I adore you. But . . .'

'But what?'

'She's a SUPERMODEL. And her father's a BILLIONAIRE.'

'I'm sure she's lovely underneath.'

'She's lovely on top. That's the point. She's probably already got a boyfriend. Several.'

'She hasn't. I checked. Crow thinks it's a good idea.'

'Crow does?'

'Yeah. You know she's always over to look at your picture books?' I treat Harry's reference to my costume library with the contempt it deserves, and ignore it. 'Well, she popped into my room one day while you were busy texting your friends. She was asking me all about the photo montage and I explained Svetlana was my future girlfriend and she thought it was great. She obviously doesn't find me quite as hideous as some relatives I could mention.'

'She's twelve. She probably thinks Barbie's a good idea.'

Harry narrows his eyes at me and I decide it's time to change the subject.

'Shall we go and find her? Where will Skye be?'

Harry guides me past all sorts of whacky creations — some of which are so weird they defy definition and others are so gorgeous I want to spend all evening staring at them.

Skye is in the middle of a throng of people. The student-types look as though they've just landed from outer-space, while their friends and parents look like they've popped in from the office. Skye has won the top textiles prize so everyone wants to be seen with her. Today, her hair is Schiapparelli pink with orange streaks. She's wearing one of Crow's new silk sculpture-dresses and vintage Vivienne Westwood platforms.

Crow is busy admiring the new experimental materials that got Skye her prize. She does not look like a girl who spent her nights five years ago avoiding being kidnapped by rebel soldiers. You'd think she was born in fashion school. She's wearing gold dungarees with a purple poncho and seems more at home here than half the students who are clustering around prize-girl.

'Look at this,' she says, in her low, quiet way. For Crow, she sounds pretty excited.

All Skye's designs have been made into clothes for crash-test dummies. Crow's pointing at a mini-dress. The fabric is silver and stiff as a thick sheet of paper, or leather, with thicker veins running through it. In some places there are holes that give it a lacy effect. It's strong and yet delicate. It would look good combined with fine lace, cotton or tough leather. It would look good if it was simply framed and hung on a wall.

'Wow.' Sometimes my fashion vocabulary is a bit

limited. But 'Wow' seems to cover it.

Skye stands beside me, pink curls bobbing.

'Glad you like it. It's a process I've developed using silk and rubber. It's such a pain to do, but I love the effect. Marc Jacobs was in earlier on and he really liked it.'

'Wow.'

'We need to talk about your friend, though,' says Skye, looking as serious as anyone can in pink hair and platforms. 'I know someone who runs a stand in Portobello and Crow's dresses are perfect for her. I've already had three people ask me tonight where I got this one.'

I nod dumbly. What I'm thinking is 'Wow'. The Portobello Road market in Notting Hill, near Crow's school, is the sort of place where top fashion people go to find unusual pieces. Kate Moss shops there. Mum shops there. It may be nearby, but it's SO not the school bazaar.

'And she needs more space to work. She keeps telling me she can't make more things because there's nowhere to put them.'

'I'm on to that,' I say, glad that I can finally sound organised and purposeful.

I'm hoping Skye will say, 'Wow', but she doesn't. She just says, 'Good'. She doesn't seem in the least surprised – as if she assumed that my job is to sort out all Crow's logistical problems. I feel slightly hurt to be so taken for granted and slightly proud that I seem so competent. Mum would be shocked. I look down at myself just to check that I haven't turned into Edie overnight, but no,

Edie wouldn't be seen dead in sequinned leggings.

We've promised Crow a lift home. When it's time to go, Harry pauses to vandalise one of the walls. At least, I catch him in the act of taking down a poster.

'What are you DOING?' I ask, sounding like Mum.

'Oh, it's OK, they've got loads,' he says. 'I have to have it. Look.'

I look. It's a poster for a design competition in honour of Yves Saint Laurent. He died recently and Mum dressed in black for days afterwards. I marked the moment with a series of orange and pink tribute outfits. Very YSL. Needless to say, Mum's black outfits included bits of actual Saint Laurent, which I thought was showing off, frankly.

'What's that got to do with Svetlana?' I ask.

'If you look at the small print, you'll see that she's the prize. At least, the winner gets the chance to design a dress for her.'

'Wow.'

I read the small print. The design has to be for a cocktail dress that embodies 'the spirit of Saint Laurent'. The winner then gets to create something original for Svetlana to wear on a catwalk during London Fashion Week.

'Cool,' I say. 'I must enter.'

'You and every design student in the country,' Harry points out. 'Everyone at St Martins will be doing it. You can try, though, kiddo. You never know.'

I decide to go ahead anyway – despite my slight handicap of not being able to draw. The story of Yves Saint Laurent's discovery is one of my top three favourite fashion moments. He entered a competition to design a cocktail dress when he was eighteen and won. Christian Dior heard about him and hired him on the spot. Three years later he was running the label. Fashion fairy tales really can happen.

True, he then had to join the army and had a nervous breakdown, but hey – no-one said fashion was easy.

Chapter 12

'Mum?'

'Mmmm?'

Mum looks up distracted from her cappuccino and her BlackBerry. It's very hard to prise her away from either when she's at home, but I've been working on this. It's time to try out my idea for helping Crow.

'You know that Cézanne exhibition?'

'Mmmm?' Her eyes are drifting back down to the BlackBerry, which is vibrating madly on the table, but I still have about three seconds before she hits a button.

'The one at the Courtauld Institute? I'd really like to go.'

Wham.

Mum looks up, BlackBerry abandoned, eyes fixing me with a Joe-Yule-like laser gaze.

'Really?'

'Yes. Absolutely. Cézanne's one of the most important Post-Impressionists, isn't he? And this is such a one-off exhibition. I really admire what he does with colour.'

I wonder if I've pushed it too far. The whole colour thing probably sounds a bit rehearsed, which it is. But luckily Mum doesn't notice. The fact is, her daughter is talking about Art. With interest. And Mum has the chance to educate me and share her passion.

'I'm free tomorrow, actually,' she says. I knew this – I've learnt how to check her BlackBerry when she's not looking. 'Would you like to go after school?'

'Fantastic! Great idea!'

Mum tries to look modest, as if she doesn't want too much praise for having thought up this incredible scheme. Which is perfect. It will work better if she thinks it's her idea.

The thing about Mum is she's in great demand. Although her 'office' is a cupboard on the top floor at home, most of the time she's somewhere else, mentally at least, being busy. She represents some really important young artists, whom she's nurtured since they were students, and they're always calling up with problems or questions; or buyers are trying to find the right piece to add to their collections; or she's arranging an exhibition or some art-related event, and it's really, *really* hard to get her undivided attention. The only times she turns the BlackBerry off are in churches and art galleries. Same thing, really, as far as she's concerned. And it's hard to have a proper conversation in a church, so if I really need to talk to her, I have to take her to a gallery.

It took me years to work this out, but since I cottoned on to it, it's made my life much easier. And I don't actually mind looking at Cézanne and stuff. He's a pretty good painter, as far as I can make out. Of course, I'll have to let Mum lecture me about him for twenty minutes or so, but once that's over I can move on to Phase Two of Project Crow.

Mum starts with a picture of the Mont Sainte-Victoire. At first glance it's just a picture of a fairly ugly mountain, but by the time Mum's finished explaining about Cézanne's ground-breaking use of colour to suggest perspective, it's become a fascinating picture of a fairly ugly mountain.

Mum pauses for breath.

'By the way,' I say, 'I've got this friend.'

'Ye-es?'

I see Mum pat her pocket for her BlackBerry, in case more important messages are arriving, but then she remembers she's switched it off.

I carry on. 'She's very talented. She needs our help.'

Mum looks at me sceptically. 'What does she do?'

'She made this.' I'm wearing a painted silk flower skirt Crow finished a few days ago. Mum's already given it a semi-approving look.

She puts her head to one side, non-committally.

'And she can draw.' I take a piece of paper out of my bag and unfold it. It's covered in Crow's sketches of dancing girls. Suddenly, Mum looks quite excited. She knows big talent when she sees it.

'And she's been asked to make clothes to sell in Portobello Road market and she needs some space to make them because she lives in a tiny flat with her aunt and she's from Africa and there's hardly any money and all the stuff is piled up everywhere and she's hardly got room to sew and I think she could be a great designer,' I finish in a rush. 'If we helped her.'

There's a silence while we look at each other. Then Mum does something entirely unexpected. She bends down and takes my cheeks (with their rubbish cheek-bones) in her hands and kisses the top of my head. I am SO small.

This is nice, but I'm not sure what it means. I gabble on.

'I mean, you help your artists all the time, so I'm sort of copying you, really, and we've got that room down-stairs that Granny uses sometimes to stay in but it's usually empty and I know your artists need it sometimes if they're staying in London but it probably wouldn't be for very long and it would really help Crow and she's so nice and Harry's met her,' I finish, rather lamely. I'm not sure why this should make any difference, but it might.

Mum takes the drawings from me and admires them for a long time.

'They're good. How old is she?'

'Twelve.'

Mum sucks in her breath as if she's just tried a scald-
ing cappuccino. Then she swears in French. One of the
words I Tipp-Exed on my Converses, in fact. French
swear-words are a leftover from her modelling days. Her
eyes keep scanning the drawings.

'So?' I ask at last.

'Certainly,' she says, smiling. 'She can have Granny's
room.'

I wait for the 'but'. This has all been far too easy. But
there isn't one. Maybe I'm better at managing my mother
than I thought. Maybe Crow just really is that talented.

Two days later, we invite Crow and Florence round for
tea. Mum takes to Crow straight away and can't help
going on about how fabulous her drawings are. Then we
take her downstairs to our basement room, which Mum
converted years ago for visitors.

We've had great fun creating space for a big worktable
and finding pieces that Crow might like to be surrounded
by when she's working: the squashy purple velvet armchair from my room, a quirky antique lamp from the
sitting room, even a tailor's dummy that Mum found in
an antique shop in Paris when she was modelling and has
lived in our spare room ever since. The bed has been
turned into a sort of sofa, with lots of colourful cushions.
And there are three hatstands and a rail for hanging
finished clothes.

When Florence sees the room, both her long-fingered

hands fly to her face and then they flutter, like butterflies, as she stands transfixed in the doorway and tries to think of something to say. Crow marches straight up to the tailor's dummy and strokes her hands over it. Then she goes to the French doors that lead to steps up to the back garden and peers up at the sky. Finally, she sits on the sofa-bed thing and puts her hands out beside her, while she admires the worktable. She nods calmly. It will do.

She doesn't say thank you for the room. Or for anything else we try and do for her. She's not big on emotional outbursts. But within hours she's returned from her tiny flat and filled the space with her treasures. Her little black sewing machine is set up on the worktable. Her finished clothes are already filling up the rail and the hatstands. Her favourite designs and inspirations are in a tall pile of paper, ready to be stuck on the large pinboards on the walls. A half-finished dress is draped on the dummy. Paper patterns cover the bed and the floor. When I pop in to check how she's getting on, she can't help smiling.

Phase Two complete.

Chapter 13

On the last day of term, Edie arranges for a video about Invisible Children in the camps in Uganda to be shown to the whole school. We watch them singing. And dancing. And making bracelets to sell. And talking about people they know who've died of AIDS. Or been killed or kidnapped. We watch some of them going to school. Most can't, because there are no schools to go to.

Our headmistress looks extremely grim and several sixth-formers can be heard sniffling into their sleeves. It's not the most fun-filled atmosphere to end the school year with, but the idea is to make us appreciate our good luck and fill the world with our noble deeds.

Afterwards, an old pupil stands up and tells us how we're connected to everyone on the planet. She tells us not to be obsessed with cheap celebrity and to make sure we do something useful with our lives.

Then Edie wins so many prizes that I have to hold

most of them for her while she goes up for more. Situation normal.

The trouble is, next morning I have to go to the airport at the crack of dawn to meet Jenny, who's fresh back from the Tokyo premiere of *Kid Code* and full of stories about cheap celebrity that she's picked up from her Hollywood friends. And however hard I try to stay noble and unobsessed, they are, frankly, FASCINATING. I'd share them, but I'm sworn to secrecy. That CIA thing you have to do when you know people who know stars.

Suffice it to say, most of the stories are about people you know from all the magazines we're not supposed to buy and some of them would make your HAIR CURL. They in no way make the world a better place, but they certainly make it entertaining.

Jenny's dying to meet Crow. She had to head off just as things were getting interesting and since then I've been keeping her up to speed with Crow's new designs, and her incredible drawings, and her new workroom in our house. Edie's been giving her updates on the reading progress and the Invisible Children video. Sadly, I think Edie is trying to compete with me on Project Crow, but I'm so winning. Not that it *is* a competition, obviously.

We meet in the workroom. Crow's in her new designer uniform of blue dungarees and slippers. When she's working, she doesn't bother with the fairy wings and tutus. Jenny is ecstatic about everything. You can tell she's been surrounded by acting types for a while. Everything is GORGEOUS or INCREDIBLE or ADORABLE. Crow just gets on with cutting a new pattern and leaves her to it.

Jenny's brought back a few cute outfits for Crow to look at. She gets them out of her bag with a flourish. Crow looks vaguely grateful, but it's hard to tell. So Jenny goes back to admiring the room. When she gets to the drawings of dancing girls, she pauses to look at them for a long, long time. You can tell she's thinking something.

'Can I watch you work?' she asks eventually.

Crow looks surprised and shrugs. Jenny takes it as a yes and curls herself up in the purple armchair where, within minutes, her jet-lagged body goes limp and we hear her gently snoring.

For a while, I watch Crow by myself. I'd offer to help, but I've tried before and everything she does is a lot more difficult than it looks. Especially cutting. She does it in long, confident strokes, but I've seen what she has to do with the fabric afterwards and if you make one tiny mistake you've ruined the whole thing. I made one tiny mistake once and she was very kind about it, but I haven't offered since.

I sometimes wonder whether it's fair to let a girl of her age work so constantly. I asked Mum one day, when she came down to the workroom with me to see how she was getting on.

'We're not exactly forcing her,' she said. 'I'd say, if

anything, it was a question of not stopping her.'

It's true. I look at her expression as she cuts. It's totally focused, but also sort of happy. She catches me watching her and gives me a quick smile.

She holds up a complicated shape that looks like a leaf that's been mauled by a caterpillar.

'What's it going to be?' I ask.

'An asymmetric bodice,' she says casually. 'With a Möbius twist on the shoulder.'

'Oh.'

What she means is a one-shouldered top where the fabric is half-twisted and joined back to front at the seam. (I SO sound like Edie.) For a girl who can hardly spell 'chair', Crow's not bad at speaking couture.

Once Jenny's had a chance to recover from her jetlag, it's time to get her to spill the beans about the Green-Eyed Sex God Mystery. I've been waiting for weeks for this moment, and I'm not going to let her escape. Since she got back I've heard every story about every A-lister she's encountered, except for one. There's a very obvious, drool-making absence from the list. I'm determined to find out why.

I'm about to invite her to the V&A café on Saturday for a chat, but instead she invites me. When she phones me up to make the date, I can hear a new tone of excitement in her voice. I want to know what it is, but she won't tell me until we're face to face. She insists we meet in the afternoon. I'm supposed to be going on a fun-run with Edie to raise money for cancer or mental illness or something, but cheap celebrity wins every time. I cancel the fun-run and I'm at my usual table at the café ten minutes before the meeting time, smoothie at the ready.

Jenny shows up in what she likes to think of as her 'don't recognise me' outfit. Since *Kid Code* went global, she gets strange looks and requests for autographs and pictures wherever she goes. However, her idea of incognito includes Tom Ford sunglasses, an enormous Louis Vuitton scarf up to her nose and one of Crow's knitted berets, complete with coloured beads. She might as well put up a neon sign saying 'I'm a celebrity, accost me.'

Sure enough, before she can sit down she has to smile for two camera-phones and autograph a paper napkin and a map of the V&A.

'At least I can still go out,' she says, joining me. 'The others can't even get past their front doors without security and an evacuation plan.'

I try and pity Hollywood's Hottest Couple and the New Teenage Sex God, but it's not working.

'So. Tell,' I command.

'OK.' She takes a deep breath. 'We've been nominated for the National Movie Awards.' She sits back expectantly, waiting for my awestruck reaction.

'What are the National Movie Awards?'

She droops slightly. 'You know. They're voted for by the public. They ask people in cinemas to vote for their favourites. They were on TV last year. Didn't you see them?'

I rack my brains, but I can't remember. She looks distinctly disappointed. Then it hits me.

'Does this mean you're going to be on TV?'

She nods. 'In September.'

'Wow! Are *you* nominated? For best kid or something?'

Jenny scoffs. 'Of course not. But Joe is. And our leading lady. And the film itself – for Best Action Adventure.'

She grins. Even though she was miserable making the film, she's still very proud of it for everyone else's sake and thinks of them all a bit like family. Weird, crazy family, but family nevertheless.

'So are they all coming over?' I ask.

She shakes her head. 'No. They're all filming. Except for Joe.'

She stops and goes strawberry. I say nothing, but give her a quizzical stare. She goes more strawberry – actually approaching raspberry by now – and tries to drink her smoothie, forgetting she's already drunk most of it and is reduced to loud gurgling noises through the straw.

I maintain my quizzical stare. Eventually she looks at me defensively.

'What? You mean Joe? What about Joe?'

'Exactly. What about him? He seemed to be avoiding you in London. You go a funny colour whenever his name is mentioned. Including by you.'

'I don't!' she protests, going totally fruits of the forest. 'And he wasn't avoiding me. You know those premieres. Everyone's busy.'

'Then why did you care so much?'

'I didn't care! I don't care! I was too busy thinking about my stupid legs.'

She's a pretty good actress, when not in front of a film camera. But she's not good enough for me. I maintain my quizzical look. It's getting a bit painful now and I think I'm developing some fairly unattractive frown lines. Plus, it's hard to drink smoothie from a straw while looking quizzical and I get a dribble of it down my chin, which ruins the effect somewhat. However, my persistence pays off.

'OK,' she says quietly, putting her glass aside. 'He kissed me.'

This, I wasn't expecting.

'He WHAT?'

I wipe smoothie off various bits of me.

'Don't make it sound so impossible. Anyway, it really was nothing. It was nearly the last day of filming. I was rubbish and I knew it. I was just chatting to him about how rubbish I was and he was saying I was fabulous and what a wonderful talent I had and all that stuff actors say all the time and he could tell I wasn't listening to a word. And then he stopped. He leant over towards me and kissed my face. Just like that.'

'Kissed it where?'

'On the set. Behind the cameras.'

'No, dummy. Where on your face?'

She looks wistful. 'On my lips, then my cheek, then my eyes, then my lips again.'

'OH. MY. GOD.'

'And then he looked at me. And I don't normally notice boys, particularly.'

'Me neither,' I agree. 'I know I'm supposed to be obsessed, but I always find myself criticising their dress sense. And they can only talk about sport. Except Harry. Or make jokes about boobs. Boobs are SO not funny.'

'Exactly. Joe's different. It doesn't really matter what he talks about. He's got that star thing. It's not just on camera. They're all like that. If they're in a room, you just want to be near them. If they look at you, their eyes bore into you. Joe's eyes are . . .'

'Internationally famous. Green lasers. I've seen them three times recently in that film of yours.'

'Uh-huh. They just melted me. I felt like a hot little puddle of liquid jelly.'

'Ew!'

'Yeah. Just so silly and . . . ridiculous. I didn't even have the sense to run away. I just sat there, going the colour I've gone now, even talking about it.' She touches a hand to her hot face. 'And then we had to shoot a scene, and the next two days were manic with last-minute filming . . .'

'. . . and you thought that maybe once things calmed

down he might start pining for you and that possibly when he saw you at the premiere he would take you in his arms and tell you that the sex-goddess girlfriend was a terrible mistake and you were the cherry tomato he'd always wanted . . .'

'There! You're making it sound impossible again. Anyway, he said nothing. Absolutely nothing. He completely ignored me. He was the only person on those carpets even close to my age and he acted as if I didn't exist. And he's a good actor.'

I change my quizzical look to puzzled. 'But he seems so nice. You must have got to him somehow.'

'Sheer embarrassment, probably.'

I think about it. I'm SO not an expert on boys. But I feel as if I know Joe after several hours spent staring into those green eyes during three screenings of *Kid Code* and a couple of catch-ups of his older films on cable TV. The plot of one of these gives me half an idea.

'You should go up to him next time,' I suggest. 'Say, "Thank you for the kiss." At least you'll take the initiative.'

'What does it mean, though?'

'I don't know. Neither will he. D'you remember *Teen Blues* about three years ago? He was the geeky guy who didn't get the girl. Anyway, the girl said something like that to the hero. He was so confused. He didn't know if she was being grateful or rude. He was hooked. It will make you a woman of mystery. Joe can't ignore you after that.'

'But it makes me sound so . . . pushy.'

I laugh. 'I bet he's used to a lot more pushy than that.'

Jenny nods. She's already told me about the fans who introduce themselves to him by lifting their tops. 'I could try. It can't make it any worse.'

'So what was it like?' I have to know. 'Before you turned to jelly, I mean? When he . . .'

There's a faraway look in her eyes.

'Lovely,' she breathes. She pauses for a long time to find the perfect description of this mega-event. 'He'd been eating Mentos, so his breath was a bit toothpasty. But other than that, really lovely.'

MENTOS?

I'm not sure I'll be reading any romantic fiction by Jenny Merritt, but I get the general idea.

We sit for a while, not talking. Then, gradually, I start picturing Jenny on that red carpet again and my skin goes goose-bumpy.

'So what are they making you wear?'

'Nothing.' She giggles. 'Well, they're not making me wear *nothing*, obviously. They just don't care any more. I think they've given up on me.'

'Fantastic! We're free! What are you going to do?'

There's a gleam in her eye.

'What do you think?'

I get the impression I'm supposed to know the answer to this one. But there are so many designers out there, I haven't got a clue.

'Go to Selfridges?'

'No, dummy. Isn't it obvious? Crow. Ever since I saw her drawings, I've been planning it. I mean, she can dress me up as a cucumber for all I care. It can't be any worse than what I've been through. But when I saw those designs in her workroom . . . Yummy! I think she can make me something really amazing. It's my contribution to helping her. My proper one.'

I give her a big smile and she sits back looking very pleased with herself. However, I can't help feeling that simply wearing one of Crow's dresses doesn't exactly measure up with teaching her to read or setting her up with workspace and materials.

Which only shows how much I know.

Chapter 14

*I*t starts with the shoes.

We're in Portobello Market, admiring the stand that's now selling Crow's skirts and dresses, thanks to Skye. Crow's been sending the stuff here for a few weeks and we've come to gawp at it, but we're out of luck.

'Sorry, loves,' says Rebecca, the stand owner, who's in skinny jeans and a peasant tunic that I suspect cost the price of a small car, 'I sold out this morning. I have a waiting list for her stock. Word's got around. I've got models who want it. Design students. Party girls. You couldn't get her to speed up production, could you?'

Rebecca seems to imagine that Crow has a roomful of people busy making up her designs. As it happens, she's made friends with some of Skye's old crowd from St Martins and they do come and help occasionally, but mostly it's just the twelve-year-old and her little sewing machine. I'm amazed she makes as much as she does.

Edie is itching to get home again, but Jenny and I are

in fashion wonderland and won't be moved. Rebecca's stand is not so much a stall as the perfect walk-in wardrobe, crammed full of vintage pieces and little one-offs by new designers. It's obviously aimed at young people with lots of parties to go to and sackfuls of money. It's all very beautiful, but the prices are eye-popping. I had no idea things from a market could ever possibly cost so much. I'm just reeling at the price of a teeny-weeny frilly top when Jenny points at a pair of vintage silver Christian Louboutin heels and gets out her wallet.

'You *are* joking?' I say.

'They're my size,' Jenny answers defensively. 'Not many are.'

'But they're over FOUR HUNDRED pounds! For old shoes that someone else's bunions have worn!'

'And they're too high!' Edie splutters. 'You'll fall over.'

'They're lovely,' she retorts. 'Honestly, Nonie, spending some of the money from this godawful film is the only thing that's made me halfway happy recently. Count yourself lucky it's not gin. And actually I'm very good in stilettos. They make my legs look longer.'

Edie and I shrug at each other. It's Jenny's money and if her mother lets her spend it, we can't stop her. Plus, it's kind of cool to have a friend who owns a pair of Christian Louboutins. I've never seen the famous red soles close up before. They're very covetable. If he ever makes a flat, cheap, boot version, with laces, I'll be sorely tempted.

* * *

I get home dying to tell everyone about the shoes, and Crow's stuff selling out at the stall, but the chance doesn't come. I find Mum in the kitchen looking all dithery and trying to remember where she's stored the bone china teacups. This can only mean one thing – and it's more momentous than Louboutins.

Granny has arrived.

I head gingerly for the sitting room and poke my head round the door.

Granny is sitting in the largest armchair with her back to the window and the light streaming through her perfect coiffure. Her posture is straight as a ruler, her ankles crossed. Her expression, as usual, is severe.

'I'm staying,' she says, 'at the Ritz. At least it has a view of the park. I notice my room here has been commandeered.'

'Hi Granny. Good to see you.'

'What are you wearing, child? You look like a Brillo pad.'

I'm in a silver net mini that Jenny brought back from LA, worn over a grey tee-shirt dress, with a silver flower in my hair. It could have been a lot worse. Granny wouldn't have liked the romper suit at all.

'Come and give me a kiss.'

I kiss her powdered cheek, with its signature smell of Arpège. Granny, I have to say, is looking good, as usual. She has first-class cheekbones, the Chatham speedy metabolism – so no spare fat – an expensive hairdresser and an innate knowledge of what suits her. Today she's in a tailored purple cotton dress accessorised with a massive turquoise necklace and purple patent Bally heels.

'Like the outfit, Granny.'

'Of course you do, darling. You have taste. Or you will shortly, when you grow out of this metallic phase. I've come to meet your friend Crow. Your mother has told me all about her. By the way, Sally's taking an age to make tea and I've been here for hours. Will *you* be so kind as to introduce me?'

I'm a bit surprised. Granny doesn't usually ask to meet my friends. She wasn't remotely interested when Jenny came back from her first trip away shooting with Hollywood's Hottest Couple, and only talks to her because she met Sir Lionel at a few house parties in the seventies. She's tried to make an effort with Edie, but having established that they don't have any friends or relatives in common, she quickly ran out of things to say. Edie thinks Granny is a certifiable loony and doesn't like to be left in a room with her, which doesn't exactly make for a great relationship. So what Granny's going to make of a little black girl who lives with her aunt in a flat off Gloucester Road, I can't imagine.

Nevertheless, I'm curious. I'm about to take Granny downstairs when I realise that Crow's been standing behind me all the time, observing Granny from the shadows with a sort of half smile. So I bring her into the room and Granny holds out her hands.

'Darling child! What a pleasure! Sally has been telling me all about you. I've been looking at those beautiful drawings you do. I sense the influence of Dior and Balenciaga. Are you a great fan of Dior?'

'Yes,' Crow whispers, sitting at Granny's feet. She doesn't know this, but it happens to be the perfect thing to do. Granny was brought up in an age when children sat at their elders' feet and looked up at them adoringly. We, of course, tend to curl up on the sofa and eye people like Granny a bit suspiciously, which doesn't go down so well.

'My mother bought one of the original New Look designs in forty-seven. Do you know,' Granny goes on, 'when I was a girl I wore Dior regularly to all the best places? Oh, those Paris fittings! What a joy!'

'Did you know Yvette Mansard?' Crow asks eagerly. 'She worked for Dior.'

'Yvette?' Granny thinks for a minute. 'In the *atelier flou*? She specialised in dresses, didn't she? She was a legend. Is she still alive? She must be ninety.'

'She's ninety-two. She's been teaching me.'

Granny smiles a huge smile and practically kisses Crow, who's succeeded where all my other friends have failed. She and Granny have a friend in common. And not only that, but a friend who reminds Granny of the happiest time in her life, before all her family money was spent on her mother's boyfriends, death taxes, repairing the roof, and educating Mum and Poor Uncle Jack (who lives in a bungalow in East Anglia, mends MG sports cars and is rumoured to Take Drugs), as we are so regularly reminded.

At this point, Mum arrives with a tray laden with china cups and saucers, teapot, milk jug and sugar bowl (Granny doesn't take sugar but is appalled if the bowl isn't included). Granny waves her away.

'Your delightful guest and I are going to visit the work-room. We have lots to talk about. Please don't disturb us.'

And off they sweep, Crow happily trailing in Granny's wake. Mum and I look at each other in mild disbelief and I help her take the tray back to the kitchen.

As usual when Granny visits, she takes over all our lives. Luckily for him, Harry's travelling in India, so he's spared the normal inquisition about his studies and his love life. Mum, however, is investigated at length about *her* love life (lack of) and pronounced SO disappointing. I'm allowed not to have one, for the time being. Instead, I become the family fetcher and carrier and have half my wardrobe vetoed as too weird or too tarty. Crow is treated like the family star.

Granny takes us all to the Ritz and gets Crow to invite Florence and Yvette Mansard too. For someone who spends a large proportion of her life complaining about the absolute lack of family funds after they were 'frittered away' by her parents and children, she always seems to have a surprising amount of cash stashed away for slap-up meals, the latest shoes and glamorous jewellery (or, as she would say, 'the basic essentials').

Yvette, it turns out, has been living quietly for years in London after moving here to live with a *girlfriend* when she retired. Yvette is totally cool. If anything, she is more amazing than Crow suggested. She and Granny reminisce for hours about the clients, the fittings, the suits, the dresses and little places in Paris they used to know. Crow laps up every word and hardly eats. Then Yvette says that Crow is one of the most talented seamstresses she's ever encountered, as well as being able to produce original designs, and Granny couldn't be nicer to her if she were a visiting maharaja.

There's a pause during the meal when the older members of the group take to sighing and looking nostalgic.

'What happened to all those clothes?' Yvette murmurs sadly.

'Oh, I've still got them,' Granny says. 'Mine and my mother's. They're heirlooms. I wasn't giving those away.'

Mum and I look startled. Mum's probably thinking of the millions of occasions she could have done with borrowing something couture-ish before her modelling career enabled her to buy some of her own. I'm thinking of all those wasted childhood holidays when I could have been checking out the clothes for ideas. Crow and Yvette look reverent, as if she's mentioned a bunch of sacred relics.

'Can I see them?' Crow whispers so quietly the words hardly make it out.

'Come and stay,' Granny says imperiously. 'Bring Nonie for company. I haven't looked at those things for years, although goodness knows my banker tells me to sell them often enough. I've got a couple of evening gowns you might find interesting. Some jackets. Some Ungaro and a bit of Chanel. Saint Laurent, of course. Unlike Mother, I wasn't always faithful to Dior. You like studying techniques, don't you, darling child? I'm sure you'll have some fun.'

Crow says nothing else for the rest of the meal. I can tell she's busy trying to imagine Granny's cache of couture. I don't think Florence says a word throughout. Mum and I are quiet too because spending time with Granny is always a bit exhausting for us. But Granny and Yvette quickly bond like old school-friends and get busy making plans to see each other again and go to a bistro Yvette knows where they make proper *café crème*.

'What about Rebecca?' I whisper to Crow in the taxi on the way back from the Ritz. 'Aren't you due to deliver another batch of dresses? You know she just sold out of the last lot.'

Crow shrugs nonchalantly and looks out of the window. I'm shocked. She can be quite ruthless when she knows what she wants. Rebecca's clients will have to wait.

If I were Crow, I'd be worried sick about letting people down, but everything seems to be remarkably simple in her world. It occurs to me that she probably won't even bother to mention that she's going away. Dogsbody over here had better do it.

I spend the rest of the journey working out the best way of breaking the bad news. Crow puts her head against the taxi window and within two minutes is asleep, clearly dreaming of Dior and smiling quietly to herself in anticipation.

Chapter 15

*B*efore we go to Granny's, Crow and Jenny come up with a design for a dress to wear at the National Film Awards that, for once, won't make her look like some sort of hunchback mutant. Yvette comes over and, with Granny in attendance, shows Crow how to pad out her tailor's dummy to Jenny's precise measurements and start fitting the pieces of calico that will form the pattern of the dress.

It's not going to be quite as loose and dreamy as the things Crow's been designing so far. It's going to have a very fitted bodice and a skirt with lots of petticoats. ('Very New Look,' in Granny's happy opinion. Dior, not High Street.) Skye and Crow go on an extended shopping trip to find the perfect silk to make it with and Jenny writes an ENORMOUS cheque for the fabric.

By the time we come back, Crow will only have two weeks to make the dress. But she seems, as ever, relaxed about managing it. I still can't quite believe we're relying on a twelve-year-old to rescue Jenny from her fashion nightmares. But the worst that can happen is that she'll look incredibly stupid on the red carpet and the boy she fancies won't talk to her and thousands of people will write nasty things about her in magazines and on the internet. And that's already happened.

I had all sorts of plans for the rest of the holidays – loads of friends to see, a festival to go to and a couple of very promising parties. But this was before Crow took over my life. Granny's house is in the depths of the country and there isn't a café or a cinema for miles. The nearest villagers probably wouldn't know a smoothie if it was piped through the tap. I predict being so thoroughly bored that I'm reduced to packing next term's Eng. Lit. syllabus so I can start on my reading.

Crow's satchel is even heavier than my bag and once I've carried it in from the car to her new room, I simply have to peek inside. It turns out she's brought her Singer sewing machine. I think it's her version of a teddy bear. And the history of the House of Dior. She's on chapter two.

Granny's home is enormous, old and crumbly. There are, for example, nine rooms that could be bedrooms, although only five of those have beds in and only three have beds in that you might ever want to sleep in. It was great for riding our bikes in when Harry and I were small, but once you've done things like wash your granny's old tights in the sink in the laundry room, it tends to lose its charm. It's also freezing, even in August. I'm glad I've brought a couple of Crow's magic Arctic-cobweb jumpers. They're super-warm and make the stay possible. I think she owes me this at least.

Most of the downstairs rooms are grand, but when we visit we tend to live in the kitchen, which was last decorated in 1972, when Granny had some spare cash that wasn't required for 'basics' like Roger Vivier evening slippers. I last visited the attics when I was about five and had no idea that two of the rooms (there are several) are floor-to-ceiling cotton bags, carefully labelled, stuffed with couture.

This is irritating. I've been asking Granny for books on Saint Laurent, Vionnet and all the greats since I was tiny and it is a known family fact that I am more than slightly interested in fashion – in fact it's practically the only thing I know anything about. Yet it's never occurred to Granny to mention that she PRACTICALLY OWNS A MUSEUM OF THE STUFF. She says casually over dinner one evening that 'being interested isn't enough, darling. You have to be able to do something with it. Otherwise I'd have every fashion student in the country round here, rummaging through my things.'

It's true. She would.

Crow is delicate and meticulous. She doesn't rummage. Each day, while Granny and I play cards and read, she goes up to the attics like she's climbing the staircase to heaven and carefully removes half-a-dozen outfits from their coverings. Her long fingers delicately trace the fabrics, the trimmings, the edgings, the seams. She's allowed to pick one outfit a day that Granny will try on for her. Granny, needless to say (and she often does), can still get into her wedding dress and anything else she wore in her twenties. She looks a bit scrawnier than she probably did then, but the fit isn't bad.

'I would have handed them on to you, darling,' she says to me, rubbing salt in the wound, 'but your mother's too tall and you're too short. It's a shame your father was so . . . *petit.*'

There isn't much Granny likes about my father. If she hadn't discovered he was the grandson of a count I'm not sure she'd ever have spoken to him. He thinks she's great, but he still calls her 'la belle dame sans merci'.

One day, about a week in, I go into the bedroom Crow's using to tell her it's teatime and get the shock of my life. A midnight-blue lace cocktail dress is lying under the window in pieces. The bodice has been separated from the skirt and several seams have been undone. Petticoats litter the area. For a moment, I feel as if I've wandered into a crime scene, and I half expect to see a chalk line around it and forensics experts crawling over it, looking for DNA.

I go in closer. The label says Dior. This is sacrilege.

Crow comes in behind me and gives me a cheerful smile.

'My God! What's Granny going to say?' I gibber.

'It's all right. She said I could,' Crow tells me calmly. 'I'm borrowing it.'

'But it's in bits.'

'Of course. I have some adjustments to make. I'm just examining the seams.'

'Examining the seams? Do you really think you'll be able to put it back together?'

She shrugs her shrug. 'Yvette will help me, but it's clear how the dress was made.'

It's clear to me how people do bungee jumping, but that doesn't mean I'd ever attempt it myself. But Crow seems to think it's perfectly natural to try and recreate the stitches of a Dior *couturière*. So does Granny, apparently. She doesn't seem remotely bothered when I nervously mention it at tea.

In the evenings, Granny reminisces about her Paris days and rumbles on about how things have changed.

'In my day, the regular clients were European princesses and American heiresses who dressed like ladies. Now it's all mobsters' molls and pop stars who dress like glorified tarts. I've lost track of the number of nipples I've seen on the catwalk. It's quite disgusting. One of them was your mother's once, Nonie. I'm not sure I ever recovered.'

Granny doesn't often talk about Mum's career. I'm starting to suspect that she might be jealous of Mum wearing all those fabulous outfits, day in day out, and getting paid to do it. Granny was born to be a model. She had the height and the pouty looks and the theatricality. She could have posed for England. But in her day, nicely brought-up girls didn't do that sort of thing. Or so Great-Grandma told her.

Crow doesn't comment. She just listens and occasionally you can see her fingertips moving, as if she's trying to remember the feel of a particular fabric. Or else she's drawing her dancing girls, but this time they're in more recognisable outfits. I can see bits of Dior and Saint Laurent, Chanel and Ungaro and others of Granny's favourites. She'll quickly sketch the outline, as she usually does, but then she'll spend ages tracing the line of a pocket, or a line of buttons, or a flash of crystal embroidery. I have a feeling that by the end of our stay she'll be able to recreate every one of those outfits from memory.

When it's time for us to go, Crow as usual doesn't bother to say thank you. She just climbs into the car beside the big basket containing the remains of the Dior dress. Granny gives me a look as I squeeze in beside her – the first time I've seen her disappointed by Crow's manners, or total lack of them.

But by the time we get home, she's been on the phone to Mum – practically in tears, Mum says, which is a first since Grandpa died. It turns out that Granny went up to her bedroom and found a new outfit on the bed. Crow had brought some purple velvet down and made Granny a new tunic dress to show off her latest jewellery. And she's guessed her measurements so perfectly from handling the clothes in the attic that she didn't even need to give her a fitting.

I think if Crow were fifty years older and a bloke, Granny would probably marry her.

Chapter 16

*I*t turns out Mum was right.

All Jenny needed was corsetry. A bodice with boning sewn into the fabric can make your curves look shapely, instead of lumpy, and can emphasise your thin bits to the max. It's not the most comfortable thing in the world, but it works. Women have been using them for centuries.

Crow's design for the National Movie Awards, is effectively a corset with a puffy skirt. As well as being not the easiest thing to wear, it's also not the easiest thing to make. The last week of the holidays is so manic with cutting, sewing, fitting, pressing and remaking that I almost forget to go to school. And that's only the *toile* – the cotton practice version of the dress that creates the pattern. Then Crow has to do the whole thing again in white silk. And just because that isn't enough of a challenge, she's decided to embroider the bodice with crystals. Yvette watches over her, approvingly, showing her shortcuts and special stitches to make the fabric do exactly what she wants.

The result is stunning. Worth every pinprick and late night. Jenny gives us a mini fashion-show the day before the awards and she doesn't look like Quasimodo any more. She looks like a movie star. She has a waist. A tiny one. And delicate ankles. And beautiful peachy skin on her shoulders. The full skirt hides her hips and thighs. The bodice makes her boobs look like they're supposed to be there. And the Louboutins are the perfect finishing touch.

The style may be inspired by the New Look, but whereas Dior relied on enough fabric in the skirt to make a large marquee, Crow has done clever things with seams and petticoats so it uses a fraction of the material and seems as light as air. The overall effect is 'Oh, this little thing? I just threw it on my perfectly proportioned body'.

Granny loves it because it makes her nostalgic. I love it because it reminds me of Marilyn Monroe, which is the direction I think Jenny should be going in with her curves. Jenny loves it because it makes her feel pretty. Crow loves it because she enjoyed every second of putting it together.

We invite Edie over for her opinion.

'You look like a princess,' she says, after some serious consideration. 'One of the better-looking ones.'

I really worry about that girl's diplomatic career.

Edie is busy gathering CV points on the night of the

awards. Crow's working. But I'm loyally standing outside the Royal Festival Hall on the South Bank of the Thames, looking at the twinkling lights over the water and waiting to see the stars arrive.

There isn't a massive crowd of us. This isn't exactly the Oscars. But there's a huge bank of photographers jostling for space. They're expecting Meryl Streep and Nicole Kidman and Kylie – so this is a night for EXPENSIVE celebrity. I now understand why I was supposed to look impressed when Jenny first mentioned this ceremony to me.

I don't see all the famous people. Some sneak in by the back door. But it doesn't matter, because I'm only here for one girl. She might not be famous enough to require sneaky entrances yet, but I don't care.

For once, I'm not nervous about how she'll look. I know she will be gorgeous. And she is. She floats along the red carpet looking stunning in her white dress and white skin, with her copper hair gleaming. The flashbulbs start to go and a paparazzo works out who she is and calls her name. Startled, she turns round and more bulbs go. Then she starts to enjoy herself, smiling properly and looking like a regular famous person having a good time.

Until suddenly her face freezes and I know instantly what she must have seen. I look around and sure enough, the tousled hair and green-laser eyes of Joe Yule have made their appearance, above an immaculate black jacket and sky-blue tie. You wouldn't think he'd only arrived a few hours ago after a killer of a flight.

Instantly, the photographers start to yell his name, but Joe is a practised hand. He comes over to the little gaggle of us and languidly signs a few autographs. He dazzles us with his smile and I could swear he looks right at me. I know what Jenny means about that jelly feeling, and I'm not even close enough to smell Mentos.

Eventually he turns to go into the building and I watch Jenny move towards him. Joe stops for a minute, surprised, and then gives her a polite kiss on the cheek. I can see her murmuring something at him. So can the people around me.

'What's that? She the new girlfriend?' someone asks.

'Nah. She was his sister in that film, remember?' says the movie buff beside me. 'Used to be fat. Scrubbed up OK tonight, though.'

I have a pretty good idea of what Jenny's just said to Joe and I watch as closely as I can to see his reaction, wishing I had a pair of binoculars or one of the photographers' massive lenses so I could get a close-up. From where I'm standing, his back seems to relax and he starts talking rapidly to Jenny. The colour floods back into her face, but not her usual raspberry. Her cheeks just look cheerfully rosy. Her face relaxes too and I realise how pretty she can be when she's happy. It only shows how strained she's been all summer.

Joe looks down and obviously says something nice about the dress. Then he puts his arm around her waist to guide her – in a gentlemanly fashion – along the last few feet of carpet. Just before they go through the doors, someone in the crowd calls their names and they both turn round again. I've never seen Jenny look so amazing. Her eyes are bright and she's positively sparkling. I hold up my phone and get a rubbish picture of her, only hoping that a professional has done a better job.

Two hours later I get a text. I'm impressed that she managed to get her mobile into the teeny diamanté clutch I found for her. The text isn't much: just a smiley face. I can't be sure whether this is because *Kid Code* has won an award, or because of Joe. I have to wait until she gets home and onto Instant Messenger before I can hear the full story.

'He said he was really sorry! He always wanted to be friends and he thought he'd blown it. He was so cute!'

'And?'

'And what?'

'Is he your boyfriend?'

'No! No no no no no no no. Just cute. And sweet. Anyway, he's too old for me.'

'Too famous.'

'Too far away, most of the time.'

'Too busy.'

'You looked great, anyway.' I decide it's time to change the subject. The I'm-glad-he's-not-my-boyfriend conversation has gone on long enough.

'Did you win anything?'

'Oh yes. Forgot to say. Best Action/Adventure and Best Performance, Female. Joe lost out, but he was OK about it. Mum let me have two glasses of champagne, so I did, but it's DISGUSTING.'

I have a feeling that if I hadn't asked, Jenny would have completely forgotten to tell me. It's just possible that her mind is still on the non-boyfriend. I hope she's as cool with it as she sounds. At least he's talking to her, which has to be good.

Next day, the picture of Joe and Jenny is in three of the papers. It's good of him, of course, but it's fabulous of Jenny. She's beautiful, elegant, young and associated with the movie they all want to talk about. Instantly, the cherry tomato is history. Jenny is completely glamorous and everyone loves her.

I cut the photo out to keep, but it turns out I don't need to bother. The picture appears, better printed, in all the celebrity magazines. What's really strange is that they even start to rewrite her career as an actress, saying what a sweet part she had in *Kid Code* and how she reminds them of Emma Watson, who plays Hermione Granger. For once, they forget to mention the father and the mistress and the spots. Instead, they want to talk about her demureness, her Marilynesque figure and her 'fabulous auburn updo'.

Her dress is attributed to a variety of designers, or put down as 'vintage'. Her shoes feature heavily in each article, however, and are correctly attributed every time.

Two weeks later, she's the opening guest on the Jonathan Ross show on BBC1. Millions of TV viewers watch her sit on the famous sofa and tell the story about the monkey and what a privilege it was to work with so many talented people. Jonathan Ross, however, has noticed that the real story is how good she suddenly looks.

'Because you had a few problems in that department, didn't you?'

Graciously, and going only slightly strawberry, she admits she did.

'But you're looking stunning tonight. Isn't she, ladies and gentlemen?'

She is. Everybody applauds. She still has the glow about her that's been there since the awards. She's wearing Granny's blue lace Dior cocktail dress, which Crow has been frantically adapting for her, and the trusty Louboutins, which by fashion maths are working out to be positively cheap. You'd think she'd spent her life in vintage couture.

All the fashion press are in agreement after this outing. Jenny Merritt is a teen style queen and they can't wait to see what she'll show up in next.

In the days that follow, her first free handbag is delivered. Then her second. And three free pairs of shoes. None of which fit Jenny's growing feet, but it's a nice gesture. Then an invitation arrives to open a ward at a children's hospital, and another to launch a soft drink. And a vast bouquet of flowers from the producers of *Kid Code*, to say 'job done'. And a one-line text from Joe Yule to say he heard she was on TV and hoped it went OK.

It's a shame you can't frame texts. I hope Jenny doesn't get carried away and embroider it on her pillow, or worse (as I've heard Sexy Girlfriend did) have it tattooed somewhere private.

HAH! I wonder what would happen if Jenny started telling that story instead of the one about the monkey.

Chapter 17

*I*t's the children's ward opening that annoys Edie the most.

She just about manages to handle the free bags and shoes and party invitations, but she says the idea of being asked to upstage a bunch of sick children just because you looked good in a frock on TV practically makes her want to throw up.

This doesn't go down well with Jenny, who accepts the invitation partly to annoy Edie and comes back from the hospital saying what a MARVELLOUS time she had and how THRILLED all the children were to see her and how the older ones were PARTICULARLY excited that she showed up in her Louboutins.

This makes Edie even crosser, because she says if there's anything worse than swanning around a children's ward like lady bountiful just because you've been on a TV sofa, it's doing it in STILETTOS. Jenny says Edie's just jealous and Edie does her most sarcastic laugh and says she wouldn't be seen dead in those magazines – they're only read by people like me – and Jenny gets a bit carried away and says that's true, we wouldn't be interested in Edie even if she were dead, and they stop talking to each other for a while and channel all communication through me.

This is not great for me because Jenny mostly wants to talk about boys. Definitely not smoky, green-eyed sex gods. Not those, oh no. Anything but those. But boys in general have suddenly become a bit of a pet subject. And Edie wants to talk about internet campaigning and her new project to help build schools for the Invisible Children in Uganda. She says her website's been getting thousands of new hits recently and (I quote) she wants to 'harness its popularity to improve awareness of the plight of displaced children in areas of conflict'.

Which is great in theory. Fabulous and worthwhile and I'm really proud of her. I've even bought a bracelet to support the campaign. I'm just not very good at statistics and campaigning methods and international organisations. I try and concentrate but my brain starts clouding over and I find myself thinking about next term's designs for my pencil case or the ideal colour combination for my next pair of Converses. I wish I wasn't so superficial but it's obviously genetic, so I don't think it can really be my fault.

But I do discover one interesting thing. I happen to be googling Jenny one evening after homework (OK, instead of homework – it's become a bit of a habit to watch the search results grow each week) and I notice that one of the most popular sites for people looking for stuff about Jenny is Edie's blog. It turns out that Edie's been describing Jenny's TV and magazine appearances alongside snarky comments about my outfits and general information about world peace and her own do-gooding.

I can't help wondering how many of the hits are down to Edie's limpid prose and biting political analysis, and how many are down to Jenny's taste in shoes.

I ask Edie about it as we're leaving school one day and she somehow manages to change the subject to how much publicity she's raised recently for Invisible Children, swiftly followed by the number of displaced people in camps in ten African countries. By the time she's finished quoting a series of very large numbers at me, I've forgotten what my original question was.

'I need to do more, though,' she says with a dramatic sigh. 'I mean, if we could get a million signatures, say, on a petition, then the Prime Minister would have to take the problem more seriously. And he could raise it at the next G8 summit. And they'd have to do something.'

'Do what, exactly?'

'Give more money to people who are trying to put families back together. Stop supporting the governments who keep the conflicts going so they daren't return home. Build more schools. Just imagine: you spend years and years in a camp with hardly any food, no education, people dying around you. There's thousands of them living like that and hardly anybody's helping them. Just because they're not being shot at any more, it doesn't mean they're out of trouble.'

I try to look encouraging.

'Oh, come on,' Edie complains. 'It's not that impossible.'

I must practise my encouraging look more.

'*You* care, don't you, Nonie?' she asks, looking doubtful for the first time.

'Of course I care,' I protest. 'But I don't know these children. They're so far away.'

Edie looks irritated.

'Huh! Jenny only has to put on a pair of silver shoes and half the country seems to know her.'

We're back on to that subject again. I make an excuse that I've got an essay on a Brontë to finish and head for home as quickly as I can. Edie goes on and on about saving the world, but if she carries on like this it's going to be practically impossible to save a friendship.

Chapter 18

It's not all celebrity and saving the world. The summer holidays are a distant memory and we have normal school things to think about too. All our teachers have been careful to explain that we have less than two years before we'll be TAKING SOME OF THE BIGGEST EXAMS OF OUR LIVES and that we should be suitably, and increasingly, stressed. It's working for Jenny and me.

Edie, on the other hand, is coasting. Take Eng. Lit. By now, she's read all our set texts for the whole year and an additional three books by each author, just to become 'fully conversant with their style'. I think that means being able to copy them at will, which she can. Her only regret is that Emily Brontë didn't *write* enough books to enable such thorough research. Emily Brontë is a bit weedy and lazy, in Edie's opinion, and should have done less wandering on the moors getting a chill and put pen to paper more often.

Oh, and there's shopping. Obviously Edie doesn't shop, so far as I've noticed. And Jenny now has FREEBIES SENT TO HER instead. But I do.

One day after school, I'm walking down Kensington High Street and I could swear I see Jenny's white dress in one of the shop windows. I look closer and realise it's a good copy. It's got the crystal embroidery and the clever cutting of the full skirt. It's not as well made, of course, and the material's not as classy, but it's still a great dress to wear to a party.

Then I see another copy, and another. Rock royalty are wearing it two sizes too large, over white cotton petticoats that peep out from under the hem. Sienna Miller is photographed in a black version on a film set. Kate Moss wears something dangerously similar under a leather jacket to go to the pub. I buy a version myself and take it home to show Crow, who immediately takes it apart, fascinated to see how it's made.

'Do you mind?' I ask her. After all, nobody's exactly asked if they can borrow the design.

'Why would I?' She looks confused. 'I always wanted to see girls wearing this shape. Anyway, now I'm doing it differently.'

She gestures round the workroom, which is full of new versions of the dress, in paper, in *toile*, in delicate pink satins. She's been learning from the pieces in Granny's attic and now all the bodices are boned and draped and fitted. The skirts still do clever petal things like before, but they also have a hidden mobile phone pocket, held in place by stays. Of course, Dior didn't do that, but he gave her ideas of how to cheat and hide stuff.

She lets me try on a dress to show me her latest invention. It's designed to look as if the sleeve has accidentally fallen off your shoulder, and there's some very clever sewing and taping on the inside to arrange the sleeve in the perfect position. The dress also gives me boobs, hips and model-length legs.

'Golly!'

'You can have it if you like,' she says, scrunching up her eyes a bit, which I know means that it's promised to a client.

'I'd better not,' I say, taking it off regretfully. It's not only that someone else needs it. It also makes me look a bit too much like a model/princess/ballerina, which is never a look I've gone for. I'm a flat-faced midget and I might as well accept it and rock the look I've got.

I'm not typical, of course. There are a lot of girls out there who are totally happy with the model/princess/ballerina look. Rebecca has a permanent waiting list for new dresses and if Crow ever has time to run off one of her Arctic-cobweb creations it goes in seconds. Several of the St Martins students require new outfits on a regular basis and pay Crow in fabrics or embellishments from their own collections. She now gets letters from girls begging her to make them something. All teenage, all leggy, all rich enough to pay eye-popping prices.

The letters provide good reading practice. Edie still practises with her every week, but they've moved on from the House of Dior to *Vogue* articles and notes from costume exhibitions. Crow seems to have missed out the Roald Dahl and Jacqueline Wilson stage entirely.

I ask Edie how Crow's getting on at school and she says that, apparently, it's better. She's still rubbish with homework, but at least she can understand what's going on in class now. The Bitches are still there, but Crow just seems to tune them out. Her head is always full of fabrics and finishes and design details that she's spotted.

At home, Mum has taken to asking Crow out whenever there's a new exhibition on.

'You don't mind, do you darling?' she asks me. 'It's just that you're much happier texting your friends and she needs the visual stimulation.'

Of course I mind. I don't text my friends THAT much. I message them, mostly. And I like seeing art. I particularly like getting a chance to chat to Mum while we're doing it. She seems to have much more free time when Crow needs something. I cope with my jealousy by having furious conversations in my head when I rant and rave to Mum about how much attention the TWELVE-YEAR-OLD is getting. I swear a lot and say some evil, unforgivable things and it makes me feel much better. Out loud, I say, 'Of course, go ahead, that's fine, you go and enjoy yourselves.' As you do.

Jenny thinks Mum is being totally selfish and unreasonable. Edie points out how hard Crow works and that she deserves some treats. Therefore hinting that I am being totally selfish and unreasonable. Crow says nothing and carries right on sewing.

Then one morning I come down to breakfast and there's a SUPERMODEL sitting at the kitchen table, chatting to Mum.

'Hi Nonie,' Mum says casually. 'This is Svetlana. She's come to pick her dress up.'

Svetlana looks up and gives me a smile. She's stunning. You could use her cheekbones to cut bread. Her honey-coloured hair tumbles past her shoulders and her golden eyes glitter and sparkle like Swarovski crystals. Her skin glows. And as she's sitting down, I can't even see most of her body, which is what she's really famous for.

I goggle.

She's eating a chocolate croissant. I'm guessing she has a metabolism like Mum's. But as soon as she's finished chewing, she says, 'Hi' and I say, 'Hi' back in a strangled voice that isn't really mine.

'I'm making toast,' Mum says, silently gesturing at a half-empty pack of chocolate croissants that were going to be for us. Svetlana's appetite is impressive.

I sit at the table and try and think of something to say, but luckily Svetlana is chatty, as well as hungry.

'I had no idea your mum was such a collector. I adore

the photographs. She's going to sell me some limited editions. No time to choose today, though. I'm supposed to be at the airport in . . .' she checks her watch, '. . . twenty-four minutes. Oops. I may have to jog through security.'

'Where are you going?' I ask politely. It's really weird watching her lips move after so many months of only seeing her in photographs.

'New York. Big party tonight. Thank God Crow got my dress done in time. I was worried she wouldn't. My fault. I only asked her last week. She's so incredible, your friend. What's her secret?'

'She actually has a family of elves working for her,' I say, with a serious expression. It's how it feels, sometimes.

Svetlana giggles. Even her giggle is honey-coloured and stunning.

Then Harry comes in, dressed in boxers and an open dressing gown, with the air of a boy who's been partying a bit and needs something restorative. I'm not sure he's entirely recovered from his India trip yet. He takes one look at Svetlana and reacts for a moment as if he's been punched in the chest. For that moment, it feels as if the air's been sucked out of the room and it's spinning. Then he breathes in, belts the dressing gown and wanders non-chalantly over to Svetlana, whom he KISSES ON BOTH CHEEKS as if he's known her for years.

'Hi,' he says. 'I'm Harry. I've heard so much about you.'

Svetlana giggles her stunning giggle again. Harry looks friendly and groggy but not outrageously impressed. He notices the crumbs on the table.

'Can I get you another croissant?'

More giggling. 'No thank you,' she says. 'Crow's told me all about you.'

'All of it true,' he says. 'So, how do you know Crow?'

He asks as if it's the most casual thing in the world, but I'm completely dying to hear the answer. How do international fashion superstars get to meet schoolgirls who make outfits in someone else's spare room?

'My friend Daisy got two of her dresses from the Portobello Road,' Svetlana explains.

She leans back and crosses one impossibly long leg over the other. Harry closes his eyes briefly and breathes through his nose.

'Daisy looked fabulous,' she goes on. 'I had to find out who she was wearing. Then I was at a meeting for the Yves Saint Laurent competition and of course, Crow was a finalist. I thought, she's the one. I must ask her for a dress. I'm going to this party in New York and it's going to be crazy. I have to have something new and she's it.'

'Wait!' I interrupt. I'm not goggling any more, I'm clutching my throbbing head. 'I'm confused. The Yves Saint Laurent competition? *Who's* a finalist?'

'Crow,' Svetlana answers, wiggling her pretty nose at me. 'The award's in a couple of weeks. Hasn't she told you?'

'The competition in Harry's room?' I ask, half to myself. (After Zoe's show, he added the poster to the rest of his Svetlana collection.) 'The one where the prize is for you to wear the dress at London Fashion Week?'

Harry has turned round to give me a furious look over Svetlana's head and I realise that mentioning the bit about his room wasn't the cleverest, but hopefully she hasn't noticed.

'Mmm,' she nods. 'Everyone was so devastated when Yves died. They wanted to do something in his memory. I never got to work for him, of course. Did you, Sally?'

Mum nods and waves a hand dismissively in the air. I can tell she doesn't want to talk about being a model about a hundred years ago with some young star who's in the middle of her career.

Harry and I have given up any hope of intelligent conversation and are back to goggling.

'What's this about your room, Harry?' Svetlana asks, with a hint of that giggle.

Harry, realising the game is up, goes down on both knees before her.

'I worship the ground you walk on,' he says. 'Crow must have told you. My room is a shrine to your heavenly body. Go out with me.'

She gives him a smile and runs a hand down his stubbly cheek.

'OK,' she says. 'As you ask so nicely. When I get back from New York. Call me.'

The door opens and Crow appears, clutching a multihued pink creation, which looks small enough to fit a doll.

'It's ready,' she says. 'Oh. I see you've met Harry.'

And gradually her face becomes one big, shy smile.

Chapter 19

A few hours later, when we've recovered from the shock of Svetlana, Crow explains about the competition.

'I saw the poster and Harry told me about it. I thought if I won, I could introduce him.'

She makes it all sound so easy.

'So what did you design?'

'I drew a little black lace cocktail dress. Very simple, but the hips are padded, so . . .'

Without thinking, she breaks off, grabs a bit of paper and a pen and draws the dress to show us what she means. It's a simple silhouette, with a fitted bodice like a lace leotard and a flared skirt. When you look closer, you realise that the hips are exaggerated, a bit like the embroidered court dress that Crow and I love so much from the V&A. In the middle, from waist to hem, is a triangle of cascading white lace. Mum, who's wandered over to have a look, puts her hand on her shoulder.

'Velazquez,' she says, nodding approvingly. 'And a touch of Watteau. Yes?'

Crow nods back. For once, I don't need Edie to translate. Mum's talking about a seventeenth-century Spanish painter and an eighteenth-century French one. Both painted women in seriously big dresses, which is the reason I remember them. I think grumpily that I would have spotted their influence sooner if Mum and Crow had bothered to take me on some of their art trips recently.

'But why didn't you tell us?' Mum asks.

Crow looks at the floor and won't say anything. We try and get the story out of her, but it's impossible. Even Harry can't get her to talk. It's Harrison Ford all over again.

It's Jenny who works it out. We're watching *Gossip Girl* and it's an advert break.

'You entered that competition, didn't you?'

'Yes,' I admit. 'With a totally genius design. In my head. Except on paper it looked a bit like a crumpled paper bag on a Bratz.'

'Well, there you are. Don't you get it?'

'Nope.'

'She didn't want to embarrass you. It's thanks to you she even found out about the competition. And you came nowhere.'

'Thanks, Jen.'

'And now she's a finalist. How many entries were there?'

I've checked. There were about ten thousand.

'She didn't want to rub it in.'

I've never thought of Crow as particularly sensitive. I've never thought of her as sensitive at all. But first I discover she's been matchmaking for Harry, successfully too. Then it seems she realises that I have feelings as well. It's a bit of a revelation.

Jenny is good at this sort of thing at the moment. In fact, she's good at everything. Even being nice to Edie, which can't be easy, after everything Edie's said about her being lady bountiful. There's been a glow about Jenny for weeks and only the most stupid friend wouldn't be able to work out why. Now seems a good time to check for developments.

'Has *he* been in touch?' I ask her, reaching across for a cookie.

'As a matter of fact, he has,' she says, handing me the last one. 'He's emailed me a bit.'

'Wow.'

'Not really,' she mumbles, with a stilted laugh. 'It's nothing amazing. You know, just general stuff. Lila's in Canada shooting something, and he's in New Mexico.'

Lila Riley is the Sexy Girlfriend. There's something about the way Jenny mentions her name.

'And?'

'Oh, nothing. He seems a bit fed up. He said how

much he enjoyed being in London. Seeing the sights.'

'Any sights in particular?'

'No,' she says.

I check her face. Fruits of the forest. Neck to temple.

'Is he coming over again?'

'Probably. In February. For the BAFTAs. If we're nominated.'

'But you will be, no? Everyone's saying *Kid Code*'s going to get every award going.'

'Maybe. Except best supporting actress, of course. But you know, they've said they'd want everyone to be there, so I'd be included, and London's my home town . . .'

Her voice is still casual. She's staring straight ahead. The fruits of the forest are dying down slightly. I'm guessing she's counting every day.

Then, during a particularly interesting part of the episode when I'm trying to concentrate, she happens to mention that it's so difficult for stars using email. Anything could get intercepted and they have to speak in code the whole time. I sense she's speaking in code herself. I wonder: what exactly is 'enjoyed seeing the sights' code for?

Later, I google Joe Yule and Lila Riley. Half the blogs say they've split up and the other half say they're the strongest teenage couple in Hollywood. Out of interest, I try googling Joe Yule and Jenny Merritt, but all I get is that picture of them at the National Movie Awards, with

Jenny in her Marilyn dress. If Joe is missing any sights in particular, nobody in the blogosphere has picked up on it.

Now that my life is full of supermodels and fashion awards I try to imagine my best friend going out with the New Teenage Sex God, thinking maybe it will be easier. It still seems totally impossible. But I wasn't on set with him that day last year and I didn't have him whispering into my ear going into the Festival Hall.

I don't know what to think, but I do know that whatever's going on at the moment, it's making Jenny so blissed-out she practically floats into school every morning. And on a cold autumn day with double geography to look forward to, that really takes some doing.

Chapter 20

*B*ack at home, Mum puts the Yves Saint Laurent award date in capitals in her BlackBerry and in red ink on the kitchen calendar, which now hangs under one of Harry's photos and beside two framed pictures of Crow's dancing girls. I haven't had anything on those walls since I was five, when I apparently grew out of my '*naïf*' style.

Granny comes up to town and insists on hearing the whole story from start to finish. She also adores the dress design.

Edie mentions the competition in her blog and has the decency to admit that she's getting far more hits now it's at least fifty per cent about fashion and less about recycling and clean water.

Jenny spends ages mentally designing the dress she'll wear to the ceremony and is horrified to hear that Crow won't be allocated enough tickets for her to go.

'But I'm her best client!' she says, petulantly.

'Apart from the supermodel,' I point out. Jenny has to admit this is probably true.

Even Harry mentions the ceremony at least once a day, as it'll be the first chance he has to meet up with Svetlana again. He's tried to fix a date with her but she seems to spend most of her life on planes and must have the carbon footprint of a major company. (Edie is appalled and blogs about this too. Hits go up exponentially. It may help that Edie puts up a few images of Svetlana to illustrate her point.)

Crow ignores us all, except for Granny. They hole up in the workroom, plotting something, and only emerge for food, school (Crow) and cigarette breaks (Granny).

On the subject of the competition, Granny is less concerned about my feelings than Crow seems to be.

'Darling, I gather you entered too.'

I admit I did.

'How sweet. Can I see the designs some time?'

'I didn't keep a copy.'

'Sweet' is not a good word in the Nonie Chatham dictionary. As soon as I can, I dig out my folderful of copies and make sure I religiously shred each one.

We don't make such a bad crowd as we get ready to go out on the big night. Mum comes downstairs in Dries Van Noten, which is very sculptural and severe, but looks good with her cheekbones, and Granny is drop-dead gorgeous in vintage velvet. Yvette Mansard is wearing an exquisite silk print dress she designed herself, although she admits Crow helped her arthritic hands with some of the tricky bits. I'm in a silver leotard (I'm still in my metallic phase) and two of Crow's original nylon skirts, which hang like delicate snowdrops – and aren't so see-through if you wear them in pairs. Crow herself is in a red brocade dress she got from a charity shop and has customised by wearing it back to front. It looks as though it's been made out of a pair of curtains, but she says there's something about the colour that makes her happy, which seems a good enough reason to choose it.

As soon as we get to the tent in Battersea Park, where they're holding the ceremony, Svetlana spots us and comes over to say hello. She's in a vintage Saint Laurent trouser suit accessorised with a long rope of pearls and is, of course, spectacular. So is the venue. The marquee has been kitted out with hundreds of white flowers and candles and tables laden with crockery and crystal. We have a big meal to get through before they announce the winner. How nervous people are expected to eat this many courses, I have no idea.

Svetlana and Harry don't seem to know what to say to each other. She's constantly being accosted by fashion people who need to kiss her several times on both cheeks and talk about how fabulous it was in Milan or Paris or New York or wherever it was they met last time. Harry knows lots of the design students from St Martins and they keep trying to sidle up to him so he'll introduce them to the supermodel. It's all a bit sticky and the rest of us quickly decide to leave them to it and go and inspect the other competition entries, to see what Crow's up against.

The six finalists' designs are on spotlit boards along one side of the marquee. Granny, who has three original Saint Laurent cocktail dresses in one of the attics after a bit of a splurge in the seventies, processes past the boards, pronouncing on each one.

'Too sexy. Too short. Too derivative. Perfect. Good effort, but too beige. Too clever for its own good.'

Crow's, naturally, is the perfect one. The good but beige one is by a St Martins student called Laslo Wiggins, whom I've met through Harry. He's one of their rising stars and, according to Harry, a total party animal. I spot him at a nearby table, and he's surrounded by a posse of admirers and dressed like an extra from *Pirates of the Caribbean*.

His table stays busy throughout the meal, which we can hardly eat. There's definitely a buzz about Laslo. Then someone says that the winner will be announced in five minutes, and lots of people get up from their places to gossip and speculate about who's won.

I'm stuck to my seat with nerves and Harry kindly keeps me company. His eyes keep flicking to Svetlana, who's sitting at the judges' table, but he just about manages to hold an intelligent conversation. Then Mum joins us. She's been chatting with various fashion insiders and journalists who are hovering around the edges of the room. She looks serious.

'Laslo's got it, hasn't he?' asks Harry.

She nods. 'Everyone says so. When they started off the judging process, before they really thought about who'd done the designs, it quickly came down to Crow and Laslo. They're obviously in a different class from the rest. And Laslo is very . . .'

'. . . beige?' I offer, quoting Granny.

Mum nods again. 'But then they realised who was who. Laslo's already practically got a contract with an Italian fashion house for next year. And Crow is, well, nobody. They were worried it would be a waste of a prize. That she'd do that one dress and that would be it. They want to use this prize to really launch someone. And they were worried she wouldn't have the technical skill.'

'But that's crazy. She's been teaching some of the students cutting methods.'

Mum throws up her hands.

'They don't know her. She's just a kid with no training. Laslo is . . . news.'

After this, I decide I can't face listening to the actual announcement. My stomach's been in knots all day and I feel a bit sick. I need some air. Granny is busy chatting up some skinny old bloke with unnaturally black hair at a front table, whom she probably knows from a house party somewhere. Mum, Yvette and Harry are all sitting miserably together at our otherwise empty table. I spot Crow, funnily enough, with Laslo's crowd of students from St Martins, looking as if she doesn't have a care in the world.

I leave the marquee by myself and wander down pathways till I find myself next to a Buddhist pagoda overlooking the river. A very pretty blonde woman in a little black dress is having a quiet cigarette at the base of the temple and waves me over to join her.

'You from the Saint Laurent thing?' she asks.

I nod glumly. She offers me a cigarette. I'm sad, but not suicidal, so I refuse.

'Laslo got it yet?' she wonders.

I shake my head. 'He's about to, though. I couldn't bear to listen.'

'Why?'

She sounds curious and friendly, and I need a shoulder to cry on. I pour out all my disappointment at the injustice of the judging.

'They're just voting for their friends, that's all. They might as well not have had a competition. Why bother? This could have been Crow's big chance. I'm not sure how many big chances you get. And the stupid thing is, she's probably made more stuff for people to actually wear than Laslo's dreamt of.'

'Oh?'

I hope she isn't Laslo's girlfriend or anything, and explain about Crow's dresses for Jenny, the Portobello stand, Svetlana – all the magazines her stuff has been printed in.

'She's been making clothes since she was eight. She works with a top Parisian seamstress. She knows all the couture finishes. She's always drawing. I worked it out once. She must have done over ten thousand designs since she got to England. She can do Dior, or Saint Laurent, or things that are so original your eyes pop. She did these.' I point down at my skirts, whose delicate petals are rippling in the night breeze.

The blonde woman nods quietly to herself. 'Actually, I think I've got a couple of dresses of hers. From that stand in Portobello. I shop there all the time. They're gorgeous little things. Fairytale frocks. And you're right. She knows how to make 'em. How do you know her?'

I tell the blonde about the school bazaar and the reading programme. 'We wanted to help her. My friend Edie's done all the work,' I say eventually. 'And Jenny's the one who wears the clothes. I'm not sure what I've done, really.'

'Oh, I am,' she says with a smile. 'I'm Amanda, by the way.' She holds out her hand and I give her mine.

'Nonie.'

'Good to meet you, Nonie. We should probably go back.'

We head for the marquee together, following the lights and noise. Inside, now that the judging's over the air of nervousness has disappeared completely and there's a party atmosphere, with some serious dancing going on.

I catch Harry's eye and do my quizzical look. He nods glumly. Across the room, Laslo's table is full of champagne bottles and drunk, happy people.

I notice that Amanda has gone over to chat to the man with black hair that Granny was talking to earlier. Granny's back at our table.

'Who's he?' I ask.

'Andy Elat. He's the main sponsor of London Fashion Week. I think that's his daughter he's talking to. He was telling me she runs the Miss Teen shops for him. People think she's a little blonde party girl but she's actually one of the most successful fashion retailers in the country. Worth millions. Very nice girl too. Your godfather Gerry knows her from various charity things she's on. Says she's a poppet.'

'Oh,' I say. 'Wow.'

'Why were you talking to him, Granny?' Harry asks.

'We had a little bet going. I asked him to tell me who my dress was by. If he got it right, I bought the next bottle of champagne. If he was wrong, he paid.'

'What did he say?'

'Saint Laurent, of course. In honour of the great man. Wouldn't you?'

We look at the dress. It's in immaculate black velvet and brilliantly cut, with a black satin ribbon holding the shoulders in place across the back and a slight cowl in the neckline to reveal an emerald satin lining. Pure YSL.

'And who won?'

'I did, obviously,' Granny says, pouring herself a fresh glass of champagne from the bottle. 'Crow and I designed this together last week.'

Andy Elat looks over and Granny raises her glass to him. He raises his in return. Amanda gives me a grin. At least I think she does.

Then Crow comes over, looking hot and sweaty and panting slightly.

'There you are. You have to come and dance,' she announces.

Harry leaps up and salutes her.

'Yes, milady.'

We all go wild on the dance floor and watch Crow do her moves. It turns out she's a surprisingly talented dancer, but Harry and I provide serious competition. It seems far too soon when Mum and Granny finally drag us home.

Chapter 21

Next day, Amanda Elat calls just as I get in from school.

'I've had a word with my dad,' she says, 'and he'd like to make your friend an offer.'

I wonder if it's possible that Andy Elat might agree to let Crow create her dress alongside Laslo Wiggins's for the catwalk show at London Fashion Week. It doesn't seem likely. Laslo would be pretty miffed to think he'd won the competition, only to have one of the other finalists up there beside him. Maybe Andy's going to let her go behind the scenes, though, to see how it's done. That would be truly amazing. I'd give anything to be there but even Mum, with all her old modelling contacts, has never managed to get me a place.

'It's about London Fashion Week,' Amanda continues, quite loudly. I realise I've gone totally silent and she's probably wondering if I'm still on the line. I nod, but this doesn't help much, so I gurgle something encouraging.

'He'd like to sponsor Crow to do a show.'

'I'm sorry?' My brain has seized up. I'm trying hard but I really can't understand what she's talking about. 'What sort of show?'

Amanda slows down and raises her voice a bit more, as if she's talking to a great-aunt with a touch of dementia. 'A collection. Her own show for the autumn/winter season. Nothing huge. Just twelve outfits. He thinks she's got something.'

I'm feeling dizzy. 'Excuse me,' I pant, while I head for the nearest chair. 'Her own show? Are you sure?'

'Yes!' I can hear the smile in Amanda's voice. 'It's actually that first dress she made for your friend Jenny that decided him, and the fact that I've got some of her stuff and so have two of his favourite models. That dress of Jenny's was copied by all the big retailers this summer. It was commercial gold. Not many designers have that. He loves the fact she can take couture ideas and make them work on the high street. And he liked it that she spent most of the evening hanging out with Laslo. She's not some quivering fashion ego. He thinks she'd be good to work with. Anyway, can you ask her and let me know what she says? And by the way, if she says yes she's going to need a mobile. We have to be able to talk to each other!'

A few minutes later, Harry sees me sitting on one of the kitchen chairs, looking dazed.

'Anything up?'

I tell him. He gives me the pitying look of an older brother whose kid sister has obviously lost it.

'Tell me exactly what she said,' he says kindly, waiting for the opportunity to point out where I got it monumentally wrong.

So we go over the conversation sentence by sentence and by the end, he looks almost as dazed as me.

'But that's impossible. She's twelve.'

'Thirteen. Her birthday was last month, remember?'

We tried to have a party for her, but she wasn't interested. Too busy sewing. We had to make do with a cake.

When Mum gets in from work we take it in turns to tell her. She has to sit down.

'London Fashion Week? A proper show? Are you sure? What does Crow say?'

I explain that we haven't told her yet. She's supposed to be at Edie's today, doing more reading practice. We've been too busy recovering from the shock to think of calling her.

'So call her,' Mum says.

I do. And much to my amazement, Edie and Crow seem to have the same reaction as each other, which is one of polite surprise, without really understanding what all the fuss is about.

Slowly, I try and explain about London Fashion Week, and the fact that twice a year this is when the top designers show their stuff for the following season, and all the big decision-makers in fashion come to watch.

'All the buyers will be there,' I say. 'And the magazine editors, and some of the biggest clients, especially the stars. And top catwalk models model the clothes. And six months later, that's what's in the shops and on the magazine covers. It's like being asked to be in the final of *Pop Idol*.'

I picture Edie and Crow sharing blank looks and try again. 'It's the fashion equivalent of getting a scholarship to Oxford. Or Harvard.'

'*Oh*,' says Edie, at last.

Crow is still silent. If I could see her, I bet she'd be shrugging. That girl can be infuriating sometimes.

Anyway, in the days that follow it's a relief that Crow seems to be taking the news in her stride. A couple of culture programmes and some fashion blogs get hold of the story that there's going to be a young teenage designer at the next Fashion Week and suddenly loads of journalists want to talk to her. Mum takes charge and treats Crow like one of her artistic protégés. She decides which journalists Crow will talk to and what type of pictures she will pose for (in the end, only one – Crow hates photos).

Jenny gives Crow hours of advice on how to handle the attention. For the photo, Granny takes Crow to her hairdresser in Mayfair to have her hair done. This is a bit of a surprise as Crow's hair is not exactly typical of his normal posh clients, but he gives her a fabulous cut that reveals, to my chagrin, that Crow, too, has cheekbones.

The resulting pieces tend to be complimentary, but short. I don't think Crow has given them much to go on and the shrugging doesn't help. Edie practically goes spare with frustration.

'You could have explained about the other stuff!' she explodes. 'You had the perfect opportunity.'

'Explained what?'

'About why you're here. About night walking. And camps. And child soldiers.'

Crow shrugs her shrug.

'I come from Kensington now. My clothes aren't about Africa. They're about Paris. And Notting Hill. And the National Gallery.'

Nevertheless, Mum cuts out the articles and starts creating a scrapbook for Crow, a bit like Jenny's only without the evil father and the house in the Cotswolds.

The only cloud on the horizon is James Lamogi. The publicity has filtered back to him in Uganda somehow, and he's worried that his daughter is 'failing to optimise her opportunities' because she's become 'dazzled by the distractions of the metropolis' and 'disturbingly obsessed by fashion and frivolity'. Thanks to his fondness for words of three syllables and over, Crow usually needs Edie to help decipher his letters, which is how we know. For the first time, I'm actually quite glad he's a long way away.

Our house fills with flowers from new admirers in the fashion business (nobody knows Crow's address, so they use mine, and Crow's mostly here anyway). One of the bigger bouquets is from Laslo Wiggins, with a note saying, 'You rock, Princess,' which in one go turns Laslo into my third fashion hero, after Vivienne Westwood and Jean Paul Gaultier. Skye drops by with an enormous cake, iced to look like the pink party dress Crow made for Svetlana.

'How did you know about that dress?' I ask her, in the middle of all the chaos of deliveries and phone calls.

'Svetlana's an old friend of mine. Known her for years. Why?'

'Oh, nothing,' I say. 'Long story.' I hesitate. 'She hasn't said anything about Harry, has she?'

'Should she have?' Skye asks, sounding surprised. That answers my question. We're interrupted while I take delivery of yet another bouquet.

'How are you coping?' Skye asks when I come back, arms laden.

'Me? I'm fine,' I say.

She gives me a searching look, then shrugs and smiles.

'You've done a great job,' she tells me. 'You should be proud of yourself. Call me if you need me.'

I'm not sure what she means, nor why, when she goes, I suddenly want to cry. I'm thrilled for Crow, of course, and proud of what we've all done to help her. I really am. Maybe I'm just tired.

Chapter 22

'She shouldn't be called Crow,' Jenny says. 'She should be Cuckoo.'

We're in my bedroom. I'm customising a nightie to make it into a party dress. Jenny's flicking through my magazines.

'She's not crazy.'

'No, dummy. Cuckoo in the nest. When was the last time your mother took you out or did the whole quality time thing?'

'There was my birthday last half term.'

My birthday was great. Mum took me to Paris on Eurostar for the day to meet up with Dad and spent the whole day being nice, which for her is a major effort. Dad tends to bring out the snarky in Mum.

'Birthdays don't count,' Jenny says dismissively. 'Apart from that.'

I try and think. Actually, I can't picture a time. But it's not as if Mum is one of those bake-a-cake mummies anyway.

'And how many times has she been out with Crow?'

Jenny has a point here. Loads of times. Every time there's a new exhibition or an artist Mum wants Crow to meet. They often take Granny along with them. But I point out that I couldn't go every time. I have homework. I do after all have VERY STRESSFUL EXAMS to prepare for, and even if I want to make the tea for a big designer some day, I'm going to need the odd qualification to prove I'm not totally useless. Those designer tea-making jobs are brutally competitive. Besides, I have to keep up. I have one friend who's suddenly developing a career in movies and another one who's a paid-up genius.

Jenny still isn't convinced, though. She's so blissfully content herself – with her little email thing going with Joe Drool – that she wants everyone else to be blissfully content too. So she spends loads of time pointing out why we're actually miserable and trying to make us do something about it.

The only way out is to change the subject. Recently, she's gone from not wanting to talk about Joe at all, to not really wanting to talk about anyone else. With me, anyway.

'What's he said?'

She's easily diverted. She drops her voice conspiratorially.

'He thinks Lila might be going out with someone in Canada. He says it's hard because if he even borrows a

Diet Coke off a girl everyone assumes he's about to marry her. It's the same for Lila. She swears she's being good, but he doesn't seem sure.'

'And Joe? Is he being good?'

She giggles.

'Well, if he's being bad, he can't be doing much of it. He spends an awful lot of time on email.'

'I thought you said it was dangerous.'

'It is. But he trusts me.'

Fruits of the forest again.

'Look,' I point out. I hate to burst her bubble, but it's been bothering me for ages. 'He's mostly in the West Coast of America, right? And you're mostly in London. Even if he . . . you know. How would it work? You couldn't do the whole thing by email.'

'No. You're right.' Jenny tries to look serious. 'But my agent's been in touch. He's had four scripts recently that might be good for me. Including one for another action movie that would be shooting in California and Hawaii.' Her eyes are alight. 'For four months next spring.'

Now a huge grin has spread across her face. She seems to have forgotten how utterly miserable she was the last time.

'And there's something else. The producers are pretty certain we're going to get nominated for the Golden Globes. They're in LA in January. And everyone's so confident about us winning stuff that they want me to go.'

'And do what?'

'Go to parties. Be nice to people. Maybe even go to the ceremony dinner thing and show off on the red carpet. I'm a bit of a style queen now, you know.'

'But you hate the red carpet!'

Jenny twirls a red curl around her finger thoughtfully.

'I used to. But, you know, in the right dress . . .'

And with the right boy . . .

This is a definite change. I can't help imagining the cherry tomato, but I realise Jenny's now thinking of the Marilyn dress, and snuggling up to Mr Drool for the photographers, and the free handbags.

After she's gone, I google Joe and Lila again. Same story. Usual rumours about both of them with other people. Jenny's name is never mentioned. For a change, I also google myself. There are more results than I'd expected, all of them related to Edie's blog, which is becoming increasingly popular.

Jenny, not surprisingly, isn't mentioning any of the Joe Yule stuff to Edie. It's not that she doesn't trust her, exactly. But if you're trying to have a relationship with a movie star it's advisable not to share it with people who write about you on the internet. As far as Edie's concerned, Jenny's current passions are Jane Eyre, netball and her new kitten called Miu Miu. (My idea. Very funny for the first couple of days but it wears off after a while. We're thinking of rechristening her Stella.)

Chapter 23

*I*n the days after the phone call from Amanda Elat, Mum's scrapbook fills up with pictures of gorgeous party girls in Crow's dresses and, now that it's colder, an increasing number of her cobweb knits. As she gets more confident, and as the money starts pouring in from Rebecca's stand, she can add more sparkle and experiment with more beautiful fabrics.

The workroom is full of pieces in every stage of production. Crow also hangs out in St Martins with the design students who are still talking to her. Many are too furious about her sudden launch into the big time to acknowledge her existence. The way they see it, some teacher's pet is getting all the attention they've worked years for. They've no idea how long Crow's been doing this. Or how hard she works. Or how good she is.

I don't see much of her, in fact, but it's hard to forget what's happening. Mum has started reminiscing about her days on the catwalk and Amanda calls or emails several times a week with ideas about sourcing fabric, or shoes, or things Crow will need to think about for the show.

Strangely, it's Edie who spots the problem. The rest of us are too caught up in the general excitement to notice.

It's lunchbreak and I'm trying to catch up on some homework. Edie, naturally, has done all of hers and is in a mood to chat.

'Explain it to me,' she says. 'This whole collection thing. I got this comment on my blog from someone in Uzbekistan asking me to describe it. And I suddenly realised. I mean, Crow makes stuff every day. Why is it so complicated?'

I put my pen down and sigh. Simultaneous equations will have to wait. This is important. How to describe it in Edie-speak?

'You know you've got great ideas about Shakespeare?'

'Yes.'

Edie is PASSIONATE about Shakespeare this term. She's INSPIRED. In fact, it's quite IMPOSSIBLE that any teenager has ever realised quite how great he is before her. She's read most of his stuff too. Thanks to her, I know more about Hamlet than I ever want or need to.

'Well, if you had to write an essay about Shakespeare, would you just write down all the stuff you've been trying to tell me recently?'

Edie considers. 'What? Just like that?'

'Uh huh.'

She laughs. 'Well, I'd have to organise it all first, of course. And there are things I'd want to emphasise, obviously. And you have to develop it so you kind of take the reader through it, and . . .'

She screeches to a stop. She's not stupid.

'You mean it's like a Shakespeare essay?'

'To you. I mean, it's your chance to tell the world about something that's really important to you. And you have half an hour, max. Crow will have much less, because her collection's really small. You have to explain your vision. You have to craft it. It's a story. And the story's about your idea of beauty. It's about the things that have inspired you, and how you've put them together in a new way. You can't just chuck up whatever happens to be lying around in your workroom.'

Edie's looking at me hard. I wonder if I'm developing a spot, or if I got something in my teeth at lunch.

'You're really into this stuff, Nonie, aren't you?' she says.

I wonder if she's criticising my superficiality again. She sees my doubtfulness and smiles.

'I mean – in a good way. You make it sound like poetry.'

'It *is* like poetry.' I'd have thought that was obvious.

'Do you mind if I quote you on my blog? As I say, people are starting to ask.'

'Go ahead.' I quite like the idea of being a fashion expert.

'Anyway,' she says as the bell goes for lessons, 'what's Crow's big idea? For her collection?'

And I realise that I don't know. In the midst of all the excitement and the phone calls and interviews and the flowers, none of us has actually thought to ask her what she's going to do.

Edie sees the doubt on my face again.

'I mean, she does have one, doesn't she?'

'Oh yes,' I say airily. 'She's bound to. She's just . . . I'll let you know. I need to talk to her about it.'

The rest of the afternoon passes in a blur, as I realise that there are only twelve weeks to go before the show, and that I very badly need to find out what's going on.

Chapter 24

When I catch up with Crow, she's sitting on the floor of the workroom in a pair of old dungarees, fairy wings and fluffy slippers, but she picks up a jumper and starts fiddling with a seam. It's made of silver thread and designed to be worn over one of her flower-petal skirts. When she's finished, she bites off the thread and hands me the jumper.

'Try this on,' she instructs me.

I do as I'm told. It drapes and folds around me like a fairy comfort blanket. Back come the boobs and hips. I've no idea how she builds them in. I check myself out in the mirror. I look about eighteen, and slightly model-ish, in a vertically challenged sort of way. Crow grabs a needle and starts making adjustments, occasionally catching my skin in the process.

'Ow!'

Crow says nothing, focused on what she's doing.

'So,' I ask casually, 'how's the collection going?'

She shrugs, catching me again.

'Ow ow ow!'

'Don't talk,' she says. 'You're distracting me.'

'But I have to. I'm sure it's under control and everything, but . . . you know . . . I haven't really heard you talk
about . . . you know . . . the show recently. Is it going OK?'

She shrugs again. The needle misses me this time.

'You *are* designing for it, aren't you?'

She avoids my eye in the mirror. It's impossible to have
this conversation in a half-finished silver jumper. I take it
off, to Crow's protests, and sit on the floor. I can feel an
icy chill down my back. It's not the lack of jumper. It's the
sense that something's wrong. And I can't help feeling
that it's my fault.

'Crow . . . You do want to do this?'

It's the question I can hardly bear to ask. I'm not
exactly sure how I get the words out. But here she is, this
only-just-thirteen-year-old, surrounded by fashion
addicts who are deciding her life for her. I've assumed –
we all have – that this would be exactly what she yearned
for, like every design student round the world. Probably
even in Uzbekistan. But maybe we were wrong.

She sits cross-legged near the window with the jumper
on her lap, examining the stitches, avoiding me.

'Because,' I swallow, 'you don't have to. Maybe we've
made a mistake. I'm sorry. I got you into this. Maybe it's
too much . . .'

'Oh, Nonie!'

She puts the jumper to one side and comes over to me. She doesn't exactly fling her arms around me, but sits right in front of me, leaning forward, with a damp sparkle in her eyes.

'This is . . . my life. In my head, all my life, I've seen these beautiful things. Now I can make them.'

She doesn't talk very much. This is a major speech for Crow. I'm very touched. But somehow, the way she says it, it sounds as if she's saying goodbye.

I can feel my own eyes welling up.

'Then why . . . ?' I'm choked up but I have to go on. 'What's wrong with showing people what you can do? Just think. They're going to give you thousands of pounds so you can design your dreams. You'll have proper models to wear them. Music. Lights.'

For an instant, Crow's face floods with delight as she imagines the moment. Then, just as quickly, her expression fades and her face is blank.

'What is it?'

She traces a shape on the carpet with her finger. Her voice is very quiet.

'In my country, people have no homes. Every day, my dad buries someone who's died of AIDS. They can't grow food. Victoria doesn't have a proper school to go to. Dad just teaches the kids sitting in a circle on the ground . . .'

Then she looks up at me. 'How can I do a collection? That money could pay for twenty schools. How can I spend it?'

I say nothing. How *can* she? I'm just a girl with a taste for Astroturf skirts and cheap celebrity. What do I know?

She points to the silver jumper. It's a hauntingly beautiful thing.

'Each time I make a piece I feel so guilty. The beauty of it buzzes in my head until I get it out. I can't help it. But to do so many . . . Amanda was telling me. Twelve outfits can mean fifty pieces. Dresses, jackets, skirts . . .' Her eyes glaze with tears. Her voice is a whisper. 'You're right. It's too much.' Suddenly she is loud and businesslike. 'My father sent me here to learn and get good grades. He doesn't want me to be a . . . flibbertigibbet. Laslo can do the collection. Will you tell Amanda?'

I picture telling Amanda. Laslo Wiggins *can't* do the collection. Laslo is beige and he isn't Crow. If she can't do it, no-one can.

I nod, but I can't bring myself to say the words. I give it one last try.

'Look. You were so lucky. Everyone was safe. Your family are OK. Isn't that fantastic? You're free. And I can help you. So can Mum. So can Amanda.'

I can't bear to think of all that talent put back in a box and subjected to the Three Bitches on a regular basis.

But her face hardens. In fact, she looks positively scary.

'Tell her,' she commands, giving me no flicker of hope.

The next day, she doesn't appear after school. Nor the day after. The silver jumper remains unfinished. Her mobile rings repeatedly in the empty workroom, unanswered, until the battery dies.

Oh great. Not only have I failed to get her to do the collection, I've managed to put her off doing anything fashion-related at all.

Inevitably, Amanda calls to check everything's OK.

'I can't get hold of Crow. She never answers that phone. She's been getting some great press recently. We've got some interesting sponsorship ideas to discuss. How's she getting on?'

I take a breath. One Two Three.

'Fine.'

I can't do it.

'Thank goodness. I was getting a bit worried. I haven't seen any definitive sketches yet.' She pauses. 'Can I pop round and see how it's going?' There's a pause while she checks her BlackBerry. 'How about next Thursday?'

Another pause. More yoga breathing. Tell her tell her.

'I think she's busy on Thursday. School thing. Saturday?'

Like two days will make all the difference.

I can hear the uncertainty in Amanda's voice. 'OK.' Pause. 'Oh yes, and can she make the other meeting? It's this Monday with the organisers. I texted her. We fixed it for the evening so it wouldn't interfere with school. They want to talk marketing and venue and things. There's quite a lot to do in advance.'

'Sure.' By now my voice is a squeak. 'Actually, she said
... she said would you mind if I go? It's just she's busy ...
designing and everything. I do the admin and ... stuff.
Marketing. Venue. And things ...'

My voice trails off. Tell her tell her. Why can't I bear to
tell her? I realise that this is probably the closest I may
ever get to a real, proper collection and I just can't spoil
the dream. Not yet. Not quite yet.

I'll go to the meeting on Monday and tell them face to
face. That would be much better. Silly to try and do
something so important over the phone. I'll tell them and
it will be over and that will be that. It'll be fine.

Amanda agrees that I can go instead of Crow. Ever
since we met, she's sort of thought of me as Crow's
manager anyway.

Later, after lots of begging on Instant Messenger, Edie
agrees to skip chess club and come and keep me
company. I'm going to need a hand to hold.

Chapter 25

*O*ver the weekend, Edie comes round to help me with geography. I'm not entirely sure why I chose to do an exam in geography when I still get the Pacific Ocean confused with the Atlantic, but it seemed the least bad option at the time.

Edie's been having no more luck with Crow than me. They're still supposed to meet every Saturday for reading practice, but Edie says that Crow keeps ducking out.

'When I do see her, I keep trying to tell her about the petition and suggesting publicity ideas, but she just shuts me out. It's as if she doesn't *want* to help.'

Then an extraordinary thing happens.

I'm busy trying to describe the impact of climate change in the Antarctic and I look over and EDIE IS SKETCHING OUT DESIGNS FOR A TEE-SHIRT.

'Have you gone MAD?' I ask. 'Are you feeling OK?'

She looks up, totally guilty.

'Oh, sorry. Got a bit distracted.'

'That's MY job. What are they, anyway?'

She's tried to put her hand over the page, but I pull the paper out from under her and have a look. She has the same level of drawing talent as me but you can see roughly what she was aiming for. The tee-shirts are pink, with a big heart in the middle and a slogan in the heart. She's been trying out different slogans.

It all comes back to literature for Edie in the end, but at least it's progress.

I do my quizzical look. She waves a hand dismissively.

'They're just ideas. For backstage tee-shirts. For if we *did* do the collection. If Crow did it, I mean. I was thinking we could use the show to highlight the Invisible Children campaign. Make fashion do something useful. Designers do it all the time, you know.'

This is the equivalent of me telling Edie that Shakespeare wrote plays.

'I'd noticed,' I say tetchily. 'Katharine Hamnett was famous for it. Vivienne Westwood's supporting prisoners at the moment. She sends models down the catwalk with placards and slogans on their knickers.'

'Stella McCartney's very anti-leather.'

'I KNOW.'

God, my friend can be annoying sometimes.

'All right. Keep your hair on. Anyway, what do you think about this?'

She shows me the latest slogan idea. Inside the heart, the words say, 'Less Fashion More Compassion'.

'It's a bit rude,' I point out. 'For a fashion show audience.'

'Well, they ought to try more. Anyway, it's sort of ironic.'

She tries a few more but that's the one we end up coming back to.

'I might get a few tee-shirts made anyway, to sell on the website,' she says eventually. We've abandoned all pretence of doing geography.

'You're going to sell stuff?'

'Not exactly. There's a company that does it for you and the money goes to your charity.'

I can't believe it. EDIE is turning into a fashion supremo and I haven't even got my tea-making job yet.

Sickening. Absolutely sickening.

Monday comes.

I'm in a room off Oxford Street. It's dark outside, but the lights from all the shops and buses give the whole area a friendly orange glow. It's an open-plan office, full of desks and abandoned computers. Most people have gone home. The five people who've stayed – some of the organisers of London Fashion week and Amanda – are perched on various chairs and table corners in a relaxed sort of way, clutching mugs of office tea. They're all looking as friendly and helpful as they possibly can. I've never been so terrified.

It's as I sit down that I realise my first mistake.

I've been concentrating so hard on what to say at this meeting that I haven't thought at all about what to wear. I've just thrown on the first things that looked vaguely clean in my wardrobe, and looking around the room, it seems that power suits with pencil skirts are in this season. Electric blue kilts, tartan tights and raspberry Arctic-cobweb wraps are not.

I cross my legs nervously, then cross them the other way. Thank goodness Edie's beside me. She, of course, is in a neat stripy skirt and co-ordinating jacket and only needs a fascinator to look perfect at a society wedding. She's also silent, which is encouraging, given her track record.

I haven't decided exactly when I'll tell them. It seems a bit sudden to just blurt it out first thing. It's probably best to wait for a gap in the conversation. Meanwhile, just for a few moments longer, I can live the dream.

After a few polite questions about school, they get down to business. Arranging a fashion show is like a cross between putting on a school play and organising a wedding, with the added complication that half the guests are there to write about it and the other half are hoping to buy something. Amanda's done it before for Miss Teen stuff, and she's offered to be Crow's mentor and guide her through the process. Soon it becomes obvious that she would be *my* mentor, because there's nothing Crow would hate more than worrying about seating arrangements and photographers. But actually, I realise, there's nothing I would love more.

The strange thing is, when they start to explain how Fashion Week works, it all makes perfect sense. I've imagined doing a collection so many times and read about so many of the famous ones that I almost feel as if I've been there. We talk about fabric suppliers, embroiderers, themes, props, models, publicity, hair and makeup, producers, studio space for making the clothes . . . The list goes on and on and I'm in heaven. Even the budget is really just a question of maths, which is one of my best subjects. Sometimes they use vocab I don't understand, but they're happy to explain it. In fact, I notice them smiling increasingly as the meeting goes on, especially Amanda.

Several times, I catch sight of Edie's leg jiggling and realise she's trying to catch my attention. When she does, she gives me the Look.

I know. I'm still waiting for the best moment to tell them. But I'm having too much fun. And then, of course, it gets too late and it would be simply embarrassing to round off our lovely chat by mentioning that by the way, Crow won't actually be doing a collection. I decide that it would be much better to do it by phone, after all. Or maybe email.

Edie jiggles until it starts to look as if she has a major problem with muscle control. As we're ushered out of the room by smiling fashionistas, she is so busy giving me the Look that she trips over the threshold and practically collapses into the landing, bashing her knee in the process. I ignore her and focus instead on shaking hands and making reassuring noises about staying in touch.

'There,' I say once we get outside, breathing in the sharp Oxford Street air. 'I think that went pretty well.'

'Apart from one MINOR DETAIL,' Edie points out, rubbing her damaged knee.

'Apart from that, obviously,' I admit.

'So? When are you going to tell them?'

'Amanda's booked to see Crow's designs on Saturday. I'll have to tell them by then.'

As I say the words, it's as if Fate has decided for me. Either something will happen by then or we'll get to Saturday and there won't be any designs and it will be the most embarrassing day of my life. Either way, it's five days away and not something to worry about now. I focus instead on catching Topshop before it closes.

'You know,' Edie concedes once we're knee deep in cute skirts and sequins, 'for someone who comes across as a complete bimbo most of the time, you made a pretty good killer-businesswoman back there.'

I think she meant it as a compliment. At least, I'm pretty sure she did.

Chapter 26

On Wednesday, I walk in from school to a wall of sound. It's coming from Harry's room. He's doing less drumming at the moment and more work as a DJ. You can practically see his room vibrate as he works on new mixes to get the party started. Mum, luckily, finds it all very 'funky and artistically interesting', so doesn't mind the decibels. Next door aren't so happy, but there's not much they can do.

I decide to ask his advice on breaking the bad news to Amanda and the Fashion Week team. Of course, I've considered asking Mum about this. For a nano-second. But it would involve explaining how I got so far into this mess and I don't really feel like doing that right now. Not to Mum, anyway. Not until I've sorted things out a bit better.

'Harry,' I say, launching into his room without knocking. He looks up from his decks, surprised. There's a sort of a house rule that says I HAVE TO KNOCK OR I'LL BE

DISOWNED, but it's pointless when the music's so loud.

'Can I talk to you?'

He considers for a minute and turns the music off. Suddenly the house is disconcertingly silent. I stand there uncomfortably and tell him about Crow's reaction to the show idea, and the meeting with Amanda, and the visit in less than a week. I start off being quite embarrassed but as I go on I get more and more frustrated with Crow. Is it *my* fault she's going to turn down this incredible chance? That she's going to waste her life? That she's stopped designing? And on top of it all, Edie had this great idea about helping the people in the camps back home, but Crow won't do it. I even tell him about the tee-shirts.

I'm expecting loads of sympathy. Loads. What I get instead is a steady look and silence, for a while.

Eventually Harry says, 'So you haven't really talked to her?'

'Well, I'm talking to her, but she's not talking back much.'

Still the odd look. I can feel the heat in my cheeks. I wonder if I'm being totally fair. Harry's super-quiet. His pupils are pin-pricks. When he talks, his voice is low and I can hear his raggedy breath.

'Crow is the one who was a Night Walker. It's her family that's stuck in a camp. But have you noticed how she never wants to talk about it?'

'Of course.'

'Perhaps she doesn't want to be constantly reminded.

Maybe it's worse than you think. It sounds like this is a project for Edie. It's some more CV points. It's a nice pink tee-shirt with a slogan. I bet it's not like that for Crow.'

Suddenly, I'm so angry I don't know what to say. Being patronised is my least favourite thing in the history of the universe. The only thing worse is being patronised by my own brother. How does he know what Crow's thinking? How does he possibly know what Edie's thinking? How can he even suggest that she's doing this for the CV points?

How did he guess the tee-shirts would be pink? Is he telepathic?

I storm out of his room and up to mine, where I instantly start messaging Edie. I leave out the bits about the tee-shirts and the CV points. Just say how angry I am that here we are trying to help this little person and SHE WON'T LET US.

To start with, Edie agrees with me, but next day at school she's not so sure.

'I've been thinking,' she says.

'Yes?'

'Have you ever really wondered why she doesn't want to talk about home?'

'Cos it was horrible?'

'What if Harry's right? What if it was worse than we thought?'

'Worse how?'

'What if the rebels actually came to her village. What if somebody died?'

'Who?'

'Look, I don't know. A friend? An auntie? Could you try asking?'

'When? I never see her any more.'

'Nor do I. She's stopped coming for reading practice.'

I promise I'll try and think of something.

When I get home, the house is empty. Harry's at college and Mum's doing whatever it is she does, wherever it is she does it when she's not in her cupboard upstairs.

It's dark and cold. Even with the lights and central heating on, it feels dark and cold. I wander into the kitchen. Mum's left a note. I wonder if it's for me and start to read it, but it's just instructions for the cleaning lady.

Which gives me an idea.

I put my coat back on and grab my keys, purse, phone and bus pass from my backpack and put them into my handbag, which is a little forties vintage thing I found in a charity shop. I wouldn't be seen dead with a new handbag. Even one of Jenny's freebie hand-me-downs.

On the Tube, I wonder if I'm doing the right thing, but I decide I don't have any choice. If this doesn't work, there isn't a Plan B. There's just hope.

The Tube takes me to Notting Hill Gate and I retrace my steps from the summer to Crow's school. It's almost empty by now. The only people there are staff catching up on marking and the cleaners. I tread nervously down a couple of corridors, following the sound of a Hoover, and get to a lady in overalls and baggy black trousers, busy finishing off a classroom.

'Do you know Florence Lamogi?' I ask.

'Lamogi?'

Then I remember that Florence got married when she came to England. I don't know what her new surname is. I'm not even certain if she still works here. To my relief, the lady suddenly clicks.

'Oh, Flo! Flo's probably upstairs right now. Science rooms. Two floors up.'

I thank her and head up the stairs as fast as I can.

Florence nearly knocks me over, heading down with a bucket full of cleaning equipment.

'Nonie! You startled me! Why are you here?'

'Hi, Florence. Sorry. It's just . . . I've got something to ask you.'

She looks at me quizzically, but doesn't answer. We both head rapidly back down the stairs, Florence in the lead and me chasing.

'I'm leaving now,' she says at last, depositing the bucket in a cupboard. 'I've got to get to my next job.'

She starts taking her overalls off and retrieving a jacket from the back of the cupboard door. I offer to go with her, and she agrees. Soon we're back out in the cold evening air.

'Er, it's about Crow,' I giggle nervously. Of course it's about Crow. Who else would it be about?

So far, so bad. I'm not sure how to put this. I've practised, but I still haven't come up with anything convincing. How do you ask someone to tell you the thing they don't want to tell you? If there is a thing they don't want to tell you, which I'm not sure about . . .

'This way,' Florence says.

We start walking rapidly back down the road towards the Tube.

'I don't want to be nosy. It's just that – I think we don't really understand. What happened before Crow came here. Exactly. I wondered . . . Actually, Edie wondered . . . When Crow was night walking . . . Well, I said it was lucky everyone was safe and she gave me a funny look. So we were wondering . . . ?'

'What?' Florence snaps, whipping her head round to look at me, but still moving quickly down the pavement, barging past anyone coming the other way. She's not her usual self at all.

I take a deep breath of cold air.

'You know the rebel soldiers . . . Did they . . . ? Did something happen to someone? A friend of hers? Or another auntie or something?'

Florence ignores me. She keeps her head down and keeps walking until we get to the station. Then she stops. A blast of warm air hits us both, coming up from the ticket hall. People bump into us as they head for home, or wherever it is they're going. An announcer claims proudly that (for once) there aren't any delays on the lines.

Just as he's talking, Florence suddenly mutters something at me, then turns to go.

I grab the back of her jacket.

'I'm sorry? I didn't hear you.'

She's looking angry and almost scared.

She mutters it one more time and then she disappears down the stairs to the Tube, as fast as she can go.

Crow's brother. I think that's what she was saying.

They took her brother.

Chapter 27

*F*our hours later, Florence is home from her second job.

We're all huddled in the little living room off Gloucester Road. There's just one light on in the kitchen. Its beams hardly reach us. For some reason, we've avoided the chairs. We're all sitting hunched up on the floor. Everyone's in tears, except Crow. I think she must have done most of her crying when she was a little girl. For the first time, I fully notice the shell she's built around herself.

Jenny and Edie agreed to join us here as soon as I called them. They're both looking shocked. Jenny's still in her pyjamas. She was getting ready for an early night and just threw a coat over herself when I called.

'You should have *told* us!' she wails, crying harder than anyone.

'We can't talk about Henry,' Florence says quietly. 'There are no words. He was the eldest child. The son.

What could we say?'

And having told us there are no words, she talks long into the evening about her adored nephew and brings out photographs of a tall, good-looking boy posing confidently for the camera, sometimes alone and sometimes with his arm protectively around his little sister. Always smiling. Always with a satchel full of books over his shoulder.

Crow sits beside her, watching from beneath hooded eyes, listening silently.

'He was thirteen. Such a good student,' Florence says. 'His father was so proud of him. He loved English Literature. He wanted to be a poet. There was an English poet called Ted Hughes and Henry loved his poems. Henry always had his head in a book. Even when there was work to be done. They used to tease him. But he got top marks at school.'

'What happened?' I hardly dare ask, but I need to know.

'Henry always used to go with Elizabeth to the town on the night walks. He looked after her very well. But then Grace had the new baby. James had to go away and Henry stayed behind to help. That's when they came.'

Crow talks for the first time, in a tiny whisper.

'When I got home the village was burning. The food was gone. The people were gone. There were . . . bodies. The school was burning. At home no-one was there. My mother was hiding with the baby. Then my father came.

We went to find my mother. He told me about Henry.'

She wipes a single tear from her cheek.

'He had to tell me so many times until I could understand.'

'Is there no chance of finding him?' Edie asks gently.

'There are so many thousands of children,' Florence says sadly, spreading her expressive hands out in front of her. 'So many camps. No telephones. James has tried for years. But no word. What can we do? We don't even know if he's alive.'

Edie looks thoughtful, but not convinced.

That night, I lie in bed thinking hard. I realise with a shock that Harry is sort of short for Henry. And that my Harry is about the same age Crow's Henry would have been. No wonder she's spent so much time with him. I wonder if he's the reason she's been coming over. I suddenly feel a bit guilty for having an older brother I love so much, even if he does patronise me. Just because he happens to be right most of the time.

Next morning is Friday. I get up early and go back to Florence's to see how Crow is.

She's in her room, already up, drawing. She doesn't look up and I shift about a bit, wondering what to say. There's an old photo on the wall above her desk that I haven't seen before, attached at an angle with a piece of Sellotape. It's Henry, his face in shadow, satchel over his shoulder, his hand resting on the arm of a little girl looking very much like Victoria does now. Her face is in shadow too, but her head is nestled securely against him. I'm guessing she's smiling.

'You must miss him so much.'

'I'd forgotten him,' she says, her pen flicking over the page. 'We never talked about him, because . . . It was like he was a strange dream. I'd forgotten his smile. How funny he was. How much he teased me.' Her voice is calm and steady. 'All this time I felt a pain, here, in my heart, but I couldn't picture him. Then last night Auntie Florence got out the photos. After you'd gone we talked about his stupid jokes. His head in those books, except when he was playing with me.'

'I'm sorry,' I butt in. 'For Edie and me. Making you try and do a show. It was so selfish. It was all about me. I don't just want to make the tea any more. I want to choose the models and get the venue right and design the invitations and meet the people and feel the buzz. I couldn't do it by myself. I needed you.'

I see it clearly now. It was always me who needed Crow.

She doesn't answer me directly.

'I've been thinking about my dad,' she says. 'Since that letter he wrote. That maybe I shouldn't work any more. Except for school work. Dad is a good person.'

I don't disagree. James Lamogi is impressive. Possibly not my ideal dinner companion, but good, definitely.

I try to be supportive.

'Designing must seem a bit . . . irrelevant compared with . . . important stuff.'

I'm not sure what I mean by 'important stuff'. I guess I mean 'Edie stuff,' compared with 'my stuff'.

'But Henry wouldn't say so.' She starts to giggle. 'Henry wasn't like my dad. He would say that Dad can be a bit of a cold fish at times. "Cold fish" was one of his favourite expressions. He would say life isn't all about work. It's about poetry and the blue of the sky. He would lift me up and spin me around him until I was dizzy and we would fall over. He was always good in school. I was never going to be good in school. Henry didn't mind.'

As she talks, she's absent-mindedly sketching a dress with a draped bodice and a waterfall skirt. Over and over again, but slightly different each time. Suddenly, she breaks off from her drawing and shakes her head, cross with herself.

'I've been so mean to you. Edie too. I knew you were just trying to help. But Edie keeps on going on about child soldiers. You know what they make them do. That's why we couldn't talk about Henry.'

I say it for her. It has to be said. I've been thinking about it too.

'Henry probably had to kill people. I know.'

Her voice is a tiny whisper.

'Yes.'

'But you still love him, don't you?'

I don't really say it as a question. More as a fact. She nods.

'Very much.'

'That's all that matters. It's not as if he *wanted* to do any of that stuff.'

'Henry? No! He's a dreamer.'

'He was just a boy. He still is.'

There's a pause. The words 'if he's alive' hover in the empty air.

'You know,' she says after a long time of silence, 'it's really nice to talk to you about Henry. He was the one who called me Crow. He got it from a poem by that man. The one Auntie Florence said.'

'I promise, whenever I call you Crow, I'll think of Henry.'

She smiles a secret smile. She's thinking about something.

'Henry would want me to do the show,' she says after a while.

This is a shock.

'I didn't mean . . . I haven't been just trying to make you change your mind,' I say, slightly appalled. 'I mean, I really understand why you don't want to.'

'That's the trouble,' she says. 'I do want to. I always did want to. Very much. Besides . . . you need me. You said so.'

She grins. The room lights up, as it always does when she's smiling. She really has the best smile of anyone I know.

Chapter 28

$\mathcal{A}$manda Elat is due to come to our house at ten on Saturday morning.

Her red Mini pulls up with a screech at five past. Crow and I are in the sitting room, watching through the window. Crow's been busy in the workroom since nine, arranging the designs she's been working on at home since she stopped coming over.

Two hours later, Amanda's sitting in our kitchen, on the chair where Svetlana sat. She's drinking home-made cappuccino and ignoring her furiously vibrating BlackBerry.

'You had me worried there,' she says with a big smile.

I try and look as though I had it under control all the time.

'Crow's a bit of a last-minute sort of person, you know.'

Amanda grins. 'She's not the only one. Believe me, in this industry, that's normal. Thank God she's got you.'

I feel my skin glow and sense I've gone one of Jenny's berry colours.

Then Amanda gets the dreamy look she's had for the past couple of hours. 'The ripped-up petal skirts. Those bodices. They're so intricate. But it's the colours I adore. So intense. Like precious stones. She must have been working on this for weeks.'

'In her head, I think she has been,' I agree. 'Months, really.'

It turns out that Crow has been inspired by Harry's photos from India and some new lacy fabric that Skye has shown her. It's complicated to make and massively expensive to buy. Without Andy Elat's sponsorship, she wouldn't be able to afford it.

'Have you thought about modelling for her?' Amanda asks.

At this, I practically fall off my chair.

'But I'm tiny! And no cheekbones. Look.'

I show her my head in profile to prove it to her. She just laughs.

'And besides, I'm going to be too busy behind the scenes. Organising everyone. You know how much there is to do.'

She gives me a funny look. I'm not sure she's convinced about the idea of a teenager running a catwalk show. But if Yves Saint Laurent could run Dior at twenty-one, I don't see why I can't manage twelve measly outfits on a catwalk. How hard can it be?

Chapter 29

*H*ard, is the answer. Harder than you'd think.

It would be less hard if we hadn't lost nearly a month of preparation time. And the days keep ticking by. Crow tries to help. She's decided to keep the collection simple and just do the kind of party dresses she's famous for. But 'simple' in Crow's world means everything will be boned and draped and often multi-layered and exquisitely finished. Luckily she's got Yvette and some of her mates from St Martins to help her cut and sew. But I still have to think about all the other bits you need to make a show work. Somewhere to do it. Some models to wear the clothes. Some way of making that place look totally magical. Some way of telling people about it . . .

Edie, meanwhile, has become super-busy on her website. I thought she was pretty active before, but she's become a crazed, excited thing. She still looks like minor royalty on Prozac, but inside she's a firecracker of ideas and determination. She even gives up chess club to make more time for Invisible Children.

I go over after school to see her at home when she could be at a club, or practising something. It's a new experience.

'I've promised Crow,' she says, 'that we won't just waste that money of Andy Elat's. If she uses it to make beautiful things, I'll use the show to help her family, and the campaign. I'll keep going with that petition I was doing, but I can't just wait for the Prime Minister.'

Edie gives a frustrated wave of her hand. The Prime Minister is SO unreliable. Despite the fact that obviously he has nothing else to worry his pretty little head about.

'So what are you going to do?'

'I'm going to raise enough money to build a school. For James, and for Victoria. Using all the publicity about Crow to get people excited. Harry can tease me about tee-shirts all he likes, but if they get the message across, I don't care.'

'He told you about the tee-shirt thing?'

'The second he saw me. He said he'd never seen you so cross with him. He asked if he could have one, actually. He said he'd wear it at his gigs.'

'But they're pink!'

'He's cool with pink.'

We pause for a minute, reflecting on how cool my brother is. Then we give each other a hug. I know Edie is secretly thanking God for her little brother Jake, who's seven. And we're both thinking about Crow getting home to her village that morning and not finding Henry there. Or the next day. Or the next.

It's cold and dark and I'm sitting on a hard chair in a badly lit room in a big, badly decorated building called Bush House, not far from Trafalgar Square. Crow's sitting next to me. For once, she's not drawing. She's kicking her feet against the legs of her chair and they're creating a regular 'thump thump thump' that coincides nicely with the thump in my head.

I've had a headache for the last half-hour. I'm not sure if it's because of the Coke I've been drinking since we got here, or the flickering striplight in the corner, or Crow's obvious nerves, which occasionally get so bad they make her shiver.

Edie has arranged for Crow to do an interview on a World Service radio programme. She's supposed to talk about the show and the Invisible Children campaign. The programme is broadcast in Africa too. It should let people know that we're thinking of them and doing what little we can to help. Hopefully it will make other people want to help too.

I can tell Crow's worried that she's going to have to talk about Henry. This is different from just talking to me. For a girl who goes around in fairy wings and jewelled hats, she's very private really, but she's being brave. It's a late-night show that goes out live, and we've been here for ages, waiting for our turn. Well, Crow's turn, really. I'm here to hold Crow's hand, which I can't do at the moment because it's gripped tightly around the seat of her chair.

At last, a young man about Harry's age puts his head round the door and says it's time. He has the gentlest of expressions, but I see a look of absolute panic in Crow's eyes. As she stands up, she sways. I realise that it's not just the thought of speaking live on the radio. I think she might be having a flashback.

This is too mean. We can't do it to her. I shake my head at the man and put my hands on her shoulders.

'It's OK,' I say. 'You don't have to go. You're fine.'

I sit her back down. She looks up at me, worried and confused.

The young man hovers, frowning and pointing at his watch.

'I'll do it.' As I say the words, I realise it's the only answer. 'Don't worry, Crow. Just go home. OK? Promise me?'

I fiddle about in my bag and find the emergency taxi money that Mum always makes me carry. I give it to her and tell the young man to ensure she's put safely in a cab as soon as possible. I promise him I'll find my own way to the studio and he anxiously leaves me to it. He can tell it's either that, or I accompany Crow and he's left with no guest for his boss to interview in a few minutes.

I feel fine until I sit in opposite the kind-looking woman with the gravelly voice who does the show. She gives me a bit of a double take. I realise this is probably not only because I'm not a black Ugandan refugee, but also because I've been experimenting with velvet hot pants, a smoking jacket and a bowler hat. I nervously remove the bowler and make myself as comfortable as I can. Which isn't very.

Things get gradually easier, though. We do various sound checks and, once I've explained what's happened to her minion, the presenter talks me through the show. It's a combination of chat and music. She's been doing it for years and quickly adapts to talking to 'friend of designer-refugee' as opposed to 'designer-refugee in person'.

She asks easy questions, like what is it about Crow's designs that makes them so special, or what it was like when she was shortlisted for the Yves Saint Laurent competition. I'm on home territory here. We talk a bit about the Invisible Children campaign. I'm not brilliant on facts and figures, but luckily she seems to know more about it than me. Then we get to talking about Henry. I do what I can. I describe the gentle boy in the old photograph. The poetry. Spinning Crow round and making her dizzy. I talk about the family, split up because they have no safe home to go to. I get in a mention for Edie's website. The presenter gives me the thumbs-up and plays some more music and it's over.

When I get home, I find Crow cuddled up on the sofa with Mum and a hot chocolate, looking shell-shocked. I realise we can't do that to her again. Mum asks how it went and I tell her I did my best. She holds out her free arm for me to snuggle in beside her.

'Well done, darling,' she whispers.

I'm amazed. The words come out as if she says it all the time, but they ring in my ears for ages.

Chapter 30

When I tell Jenny about the experience, for once her jaw doesn't hit the floor. In fact, she looks pretty unimpressed. Turns out, she did two newspaper interviews yesterday about *Kid Code* and she's got a TV one for some satellite channel tomorrow. At the moment, interviews for Jenny are no big deal.

It's the end of the year and that means the big award nominations season. The *Kid Code* PR people have gone into overdrive, finding opportunities for all the stars to remind everyone about the movie. So she's as busy as the rest of us, telling people the monkey story and gushing about how talented everybody was. She's particularly gushy when she talks about her green-eyed co-star, but as the rest of the world is just as gushy whenever his name is mentioned, this doesn't strike anyone as odd, luckily.

It's a strange effect of our busyness, but as we all cram the last few weeks of school in between more important stuff, we seem to get better at it. Florence hasn't had a despairing note from Crow's teacher for ages. Edie's end-of-term report says her work is 'more thoughtful and mature' than before, when it was merely perfect. My essay on *Jane Eyre* (written between a choreography plan and several begging letters for props and fabric) comes second only to Jenny's. Her insight into the growing relationship between Jane and Mr Rochester is said to be 'particularly perceptive'. Can't imagine why. Our Eng. Lit. teacher's very impressed with our diligent approach.

Soon after, though, Jenny's diligent approach goes out of the window.

It's the end of term and the announcement of the Golden Globe nominations. As soon as she gets the call from her agent, we cluster round to hear the news. *Kid Code* is near the top of the list, with five. If there was an award for Best Performance By A Pair Of Laser Green Eyes, it would be six.

That evening, there's a birthday party to go to. Jenny corners me the second I arrive, while I'm busy taking my jacket off, and half whispers, half shouts.

'He's invited me to the Globes!'

'Who? Joe?'

She grins like the Cheshire Cat.

'But you're going anyway.' I'm confused.

'No, dummy, AS HIS DATE. He says Lila can't make it. His mum's been a million times. He wanted to know if I'd mind standing beside him for photos and stuff.'

I dump my jacket on top of the pile. I usually wear my pink fake polar bear one to these things. It's the only way to find it afterwards.

'Date? Was it code?' I'm still confused.

'You tell me.'

Her grin says she knows the answer.

'So let me get this right. You're going to be standing on the red carpet. Next to THE NEW TEENAGE SEX GOD. As his DATE?'

'Shhhh. Don't tell anyone.' Giggle. 'And there's something else.'

'What? George Clooney wants to adopt you?'

'Not quite. Chanel. Are. Offering. Me. A. Dress. I'm going along to choose one next week.'

I sit on the coat pile, hard. It collapses on to the floor. As do I.

Several Tipp-Ex words from the Converses suggest themselves, in multiple languages.

After a deep breath, I try it again.

'OK. You're going with Joe Yule. As his date. IN CHANEL.'

Even saying it out loud, it still doesn't sound right.

Two new arrivals come into the room, see me on the coats on the floor, give me a filthy look and chuck their outerwear at me. Jenny, fashion plate and date to the stars, is kind enough to help me sort it all out.

'We have to tell Edie,' I say eventually. 'I can't keep this to myself.'

'Go ahead,' Jenny grins. 'I mean, Joe will be telling his fans and . . . people.'

She looks as if she's about to levitate with happiness.

Edie arrives late at the party. Orchestra performance. I spot her in the crowd and tell her. Like me, she takes a while to process the news. Even then, she looks totally unconvinced.

'I'm sorry. I love Jenny as much as you do, but, you know, she's Jenny and Joe's a movie star. He's got the pick of practically anyone in the world. And he's got a girl-friend.'

As soon as I get home, I look up the last Chanel autumn/winter collection on YouTube. It's very beautiful, of course. All greys and silvers and black. Fabulous proportions. Totally elegant. Very *My Fair Lady*.

I can't imagine Jenny in any of it, but my brain is probably still clouded by the cherry tomato and the yellow trouser suit.

While I'm on my laptop, I google Joe again for clues. The internet is suddenly full of stories about the break-up of Joe and Lila Riley.

'Lila in tears as friends call to comfort her'

'Joe Drool announces: it's over'

'Lila says, It was me who called it off'

'Who's the stunning co-star they say has caught the attention of Hollywood's hottest heart-throb? Rumour has it that the teenage love-god has fallen hook, line and sinker for a secret sex-pot he met on-set'

'There was no-one else,' announces a spokesman for Joe and Lila. 'Due to our work commitments, we have decided to give each other space. That is all we have to say.'

In my dream that night, Jenny *is* a cherry tomato, and Karl Lagerfeld is walking up the red carpet with her. He waves his fan around and accidentally squashes her. Edie's posing for photographers with her arm around Joe Yule, who's dressed as a knight on a chessboard. I'm frantically telling everyone that they're not supposed to be there. I'm so glad when I wake up.

Chapter 31

*W*e never listen to the World Service, but obviously a lot of other people do. Millions. The producer calls a few days after my broadcast to say they can't believe how many calls and emails they've had from people who were touched by Crow's story and want to help. Edie's website is so overwhelmed it crashes for a while (which you'd think would be annoying but actually makes her even smugger than when she got 100% in maths last year).

It's not all about child soldiers, though. As each day goes by, more messages come in wishing Crow luck for London Fashion Week. Including the ones from Uganda. It turns out that there are just as many budding fashion designers in Kampala as there are in Kensington. Who knew?

As Crow becomes a bit of a celebrity, rumours about Henry Lamogi suddenly start springing up all over the place. People who work in the camps, or people who know people who've been there, all seem to have an opinion. He's still in the army. He's dead. He's wounded. He's mute and he's writing poetry in a camp near the border. He's escaped to Kenya. He's living in New York.

The news filters back to Edie via her site, but the experts she talks to keep telling her not to believe any of it. Rumours in war zones are dangerous things and totally unreliable. We have to ignore them all. And naturally, we don't tell Crow. Even Edie doesn't.

We don't tell Jenny, either. And she doesn't ask, because she's got other things on her mind, which is understandable.

The week before Christmas, I meet up with her at the V&A, on the way home from her visit to Chanel. The café's full of people resting their feet after some heavy Christmas shopping down the road in Knightsbridge. Harrods bags everywhere and hardly a place to sit. As usual, I'm early and she's late.

'How did it go?' I ask, as soon as I spot the Louis Vuitton scarf and the sunglasses.

She pauses to smile at the table of Japanese tourists who are grinning at her and mouthing 'Kid Code' enthusiastically.

'It was a bit depressing, actually,' she says lightly, de-scarfing herself. 'I mean, I'm not typical model size. I didn't exactly have the pick of the collection. We chose this one.'

She shows me a picture on her phone of a pale-grey, knee-length confection with about a million pleats and scattered feathers. 'But it's going to take some serious adjusting. We could only just get it over my boobs. And they had to unpick a bit to make it fit my hips. But I'm going on a major diet. And I'm getting some new Louboutins. It'll be fabulous.'

But she doesn't want to talk about the CHANEL DRESSES she's just been trying on. She wants to talk about Joe and the rumours about the secret glamorous co-star.

'See?' she says.

I'm starting to believe it. After all, Jenny was all over the papers a couple of months ago, looking gorgeous every time.

'And I've got a screen test tomorrow,' she continues happily. 'For that Hawaii movie I told you about.'

'Screen test? Does that mean you're going to California *now*?'

'No. Soho. They're just going to film me saying some of the lines. Lots of people are doing it. They want to test my screen chemistry with Toby Linehan.'

Toby Linehan was a house-elf in Harry Potter. He's not exactly Joe Yule, but she's got quite enough chemistry going on there already.

'Who do you play?'

'Well . . .' She sounds a bit embarrassed. 'It's a girl who's the cousin of this boy who can decipher Ancient

Greek messages. They have to race around the world looking for this lost city.'

It sounds as though they've taken the script of *Kid Code*, done a word search for Egypt and swapped it for Greece.

'Great!' I lie. 'Sounds fantastic.'

Later I text Edie and we agree what a really bad idea it is and how she'll probably live to regret it.

Chapter 32

*W*ith the holidays underway, Crow's spending a lot of time in her new studio, which is in an old school in Battersea. Basically, it could be Pablo Dodo's warehouse in Hoxton, but transported to the other side of London. Inside, it's just as plain and industrial, but obviously covered in much more attractive designs. And I have insisted on at least one comfortable chair.

In between dress designs, Edie's persuaded Crow to have a look at the 'Less Fashion More Compassion' logo. With a few flicks of her pen she transforms the heart shape, making it up out of mini pictures of her dancing girls, all black and big-haired, like her, and having a seriously good time. We like to think it's how the Invisible Children would be, if they had places to go home to.

We all love it.

'We can put it on the programmes too,' I say. 'And the goodie bags.'

I make a note in my book. I now carry a notebook

around with me wherever I go, because it is INCRED-
IBLE how much stuff needs to be organised for Crow's
six minutes in the limelight and every time one of us has
a good idea it needs to go somewhere. Mum is jokingly
talking about getting me a BlackBerry for Christmas, but
that would be too sad for words.

Thinking about it, it would be useful, though.

This year, Christmas is not the mega-event it usually is. It
sort of comes and goes in the middle of all the preparations. However, we do find time for presents. Crow gives
me the silver jumper. It turns out she was always going to
give it to me, even when she wasn't talking to me.

'My God!' Mum says. 'You've got a figure!'

I know. It's amazing what proper clothes can do.

I give Crow a book of poems by Ted Hughes. It
includes the poems that got her her nickname. I would-
n't say she exactly buries herself in it, but she seems
pleased to have it near her, all the same. She puts it in her
satchel and keeps it there.

Jenny and Edie's presents to each other are more like
peace offerings. Jenny puts a chunk of her *Kid Code*
money into Edie's campaign. And Edie gives Jenny a pair
of silver roses on clips (found by me in Portobello) to
cheer up her old Louboutins. Edie is really very thoughtful under all the Edie-ness.

Throughout the holidays, Amanda Elat is constantly on

the phone with ideas and suggestions. She's impressed with the amount of publicity we're getting and has donated a seriously generous amount of money already to Edie's campaign. And she doesn't mind the fact that the 'Less Fashion More Compassion' logo will be as big as the Miss Teen one at Crow's show. And this despite the fact that Miss Teen exists to sell fashion to teenagers and would look pretty silly if we all started giving all our money to charity and stopped spending it on cute little tops and cut-offs.

Thanks to Amanda, people keep on offering us favours, so we can stretch the budget. Which, frankly, needs all the stretching it can get, because while it initially seemed HUGE it's amazing how quickly it can get guzzled up by silk, shoes, printing, studio hire and all the rest, even though we're doing loads of the jobs ourselves. When I eventually get married I am seriously going to elope. Organising a big occasion is just crazy.

Anyway, usually when she rings Amanda is fairly excited about some idea she's had, but one day I get a call and she sounds like Jenny on helium.

'Big news,' she announces. 'DJ Rémi has said he's going to do the music for Crow's show. He's an old friend of mine. You'll love him.'

'Fantastic,' I tell her, desperate to google DJ Rémi the minute she's off the line. 'Thank you.'

'He's in town for New Year. He's offered to come to the

studio to get an idea of the collection. Be very, very nice to him. He's a bit of a superstar.'

She gives me a number and I promise faithfully to call. When I google DJ Rémi, I realise I was right to sound impressed. He is THE DJ that everyone wants for all the shows. Lagerfeld loves him. Galliano went to his last birthday party. Donatella Versace has him on speed dial.

I sort of wish I hadn't googled him, actually. My voice is a squeak when I make the call. I can't really believe it when he casually agrees to pop round to the studio to talk to us.

What's more, when he comes over to Battersea, he LOVES the collection, which is set out in a series of bold designs all over the walls.

'Ze skirts – ze pouff. So party. So feminine. Ze lace. Ze colours. So STRONG.'

They *are* strong. Jewel colours: emerald, sapphire, amethyst and ruby; silver and gold. They glow and shimmer.

He strolls around in his black leather coat and trousers, looking like an overgrown wallet, touching and enthusing. I follow like a puppy, not sure what to do. Crow stays where she is, at her design table, head cocked. Waiting.

Then he whips out an iPod, fits it into our speakers and starts running through a list of ideas.

'I am INSPIRED. You need NEW. You need PARTY.

You need HOUSE. You need ATMOSPHERE. Listen to ZEES.'

He rapidly flicks through a dozen tracks, all with a heavy bass beat, all played at full volume. All mixed to within an inch of their lives and overlaid with strange sound effects, like jet engines taking off and raindrops on a tin roof.

Crow gives me a look.

I can tell she doesn't like it. I shrug helplessly. Donatella Versace has him on speed dial.

The look gets stronger.

'Erm, actually, while we've been working on the collection we've been listening to some older stuff,' I explain. 'Like David Bowie. And Ella Fitzgerald. And . . . er . . . Chopin.'

DJ Rémi looks up from his iPod and gives me a long, appraising glance. I look down at myself and wish that for once I had dressed like a grown-up. Sure, these are my favourite leggings and my Converses still make me smile. But I'm all flowery and girly and I happen to have decided on a smocked dress this morning that makes me look about four. The only grown-up thing I'm wearing is my bowler hat and I'm not sure, in the circumstances, it's quite right for the effect I'm going for. I need to smarten up my act if I'm going to keep working with Crow.

'Chopin?'

'Yes. A sort of ballet vibe. It was my brother's idea.'

'Your brother is a DJ?'

'Yes, actually. Sometimes.' I bite my lip.

'Sometimes?'

'Well, he's really a photographer. But he gave us loads of ideas for the collection. They've really helped.'

'He has done music for a show before? He knows what they used at Dior? At Donna Karan?'

'Er . . . no.'

Crow has turned her back on us. She's returned to working on a *toile*. Her back is an instruction to me. I know what she means, but I really wish she didn't.

'So. You don't like house music?'

'It's not exactly that. It's just, we wanted something more romantic.' I realise that I am translating Crow's shoulders. They relax slightly and I know that I've got it right. Then I understand what she really wants.

'Actually, thank you so much for coming, but I think we'll probably, er, stick with my brother. You know. He's kind of . . . been helping us since the collection started. He's sort of . . . got it.'

DJ Rémi pulls himself up to his full leather-coated height.

'I am DJ Rémi,' he points out.

'Oh, definitely.'

'I'm a busy, busy person. Amanda asked me to come here as a favour. I could be in a bar right now, sipping COCKTAILS. Instead I am here. If I leave now, I LEAVE. For good.'

'Oh, right. I'm *really* sorry.'

I realise that I'm winding one leg around the other and that I've subconsciously channelled the look of the piano player in *High School Musical* and I feel utterly ridiculous. I notice Crow's shoulders moving slightly and realise that she is silently giggling. I could kill her.

'Do not concern yourself,' DJ Rémi says haughtily, removing his iPod from the speakers with a flourish. 'They say never work with infants, you know? I will think of it as a lucky escape.'

When I tell Amanda, she's gobsmacked. There is silence down the line for a long time. Then she laughs so hard she can hardly speak, and says she only wishes she could have been there. And that it's a big commitment for Harry to take on and very kind of him to agree to it. Which is when I remember that we haven't actually asked him yet. I keep this to myself.

As usual, Crow hardly mentions it. She just gives me a wide smile and gets on with perfecting one of the outfits. Next time I turn up at the studio, though, there's a piece I haven't seen before. A mini dress, made out of cast-off bits of lace and silk, with knitted cobweb sleeves. It's a work of art. My size. I'm not sure whether to wear it or frame it. Crow grins as I try it on. As a way of saying thank you, it works for me.

Luckily, Harry says yes to doing the show. He seems to have all sorts of interesting tracks lined up already. It's as if he was waiting to be asked.

Chapter 33

*E*die is amazing and if she doesn't make the United Nations she may end up as a saint. Thanks to her getting everyone talking about Crow's village and the boys who were taken in the raid, two of them have been tracked down by charity workers in Northern Uganda. Funnily enough, although I'm ready and waiting for her to be SUPER-SMUG at the news, she isn't at all. One hundred per cent in maths? Insufferable. Two boys reunited with their families? Really humble and sweet. She only mentions it in passing.

I'm totally proud of her. However, after a while I sense that something's wrong.

We're getting ready to go back to school, but instead of cheerfully reeling off all the stuff she's read over the holidays and saying how much she's looking forward to all her clubs, she's gone all glum and silent.

Jenny's too busy planning what to wear with her CHANEL DRESS to impress her BOYFRIEND to notice, but I do.

'Out with it,' I demand.

At first Edie pretends there's nothing to come out with. Then she starts looking guilty.

'You mustn't tell Crow,' she says.

'Tell her what?

'Promise you won't say.'

'I can keep a secret.'

Honestly. Edie. She thinks that just because she has to tell the world exactly what she's thinking at any given moment, none of us are capable of keeping our thoughts to ourselves.

Anyway, regardless of what she thinks, she *is* incapable of keeping a secret. So she tells me.

'You know those boys they found? One of them knows what really happened to Henry. He was with him in a raid a couple of years ago.'

'And?'

She sighs. 'They were ambushed. Henry got shot in the head and they had to leave him behind. This boy doesn't even know where he's buried.'

'Oh.'

'Don't tell Crow yet.'

'Of course not! Anyway, it could be another rumour,' I say hopefully.

She shakes her head. This is different. This time there's a witness. And life isn't that kind.

'So when are we going to tell her?'

'It's not up to us. They're still checking it out. Then I guess James will tell her.'

It's easy to keep the secret with Jenny. The Golden Globes are in a few days' time and Jenny can't think about anything that isn't a diet, a fitness session, a Hollywood party schedule or a name beginning with J and ending with -oe Yule. I've been kind of giving her a bit of space myself recently, because this can get a little boring after a while. And she seems to think that me talking constantly about makeup designs and choreography and seating plans is pretty boring too (no idea why). But now I want to take my mind off Edie's news, so I'm happy to indulge Jenny by talking about Mr Drool.

The first time she'll see him is at a party for the *Kid Code* stars and crew, the night before the big event. The party itself will be a big occasion, because Hollywood's Hottest Couple will be there, along with some of their A-list mates. Jenny knows she has to make an impact, so she's packing the Dior cocktail dress that she wore on the Jonathan Ross show, and that brought her such good luck. She's spent hours working out how to perfect her makeup and got Granny's hairdresser to give her a short, new haircut that reveals EVEN JENNY has cheekbones. I'm gutted.

We spend an afternoon in Selfridges, choosing perfume. She wants to be mysterious and subtle, but also stand out in a crowd. By the time we've driven four sales assistants to the point of madness with her demands, we both smell like an air freshener disaster and settle for the one with the most attractive bottle.

I pack her off to the airport with a playlist of inspirational music, courtesy of Harry, and a promise to watch every red-carpet second of her in Chanel on cable. She's so excited she can hardly speak.

'Think of me tomorrow night,' she says.

Tomorrow night is *Kid Code* party night. I promise I will. It'll be hard not to. I make her promise to text me as soon as she gets back to her hotel and tell me how it went.

'Tomorrow night' in California is early morning in London. I leave my phone beside the bed. But when I wake up, with light pouring through the window, there's still no text. I wait all morning. No text. My mind runs through a thousand possibilities. Some are very inappropriate for a nearly-fifteen-year-old. Some are dreadful. But the most likely explanation is that Jenny was having such a good time that she forgot.

Thank goodness for the internet. I google the *Kid Code* party and wait to see what the gossip is. Does it, for example, include any interesting updates on the love life of a certain Mr Yule?

It does. There's even a picture of the stars and their dates, posing for the paparazzi.

In the foreground, Joe looks like he's having the time of his life. Beside him is a girl beaming happily and posing in her designer dress.

'Joe Yule looking loved-up beside his new squeeze, the rising starlet, Sigrid Santorini.'

In the background, I can just about make out Jenny, in her Dior, looking as if she's been hit by a bus.

Sigrid Santorini starred in a Spanish film last year that won Best Foreign Film at the Oscars. She is part Swedish, part Spanish, part Italian and one hundred per cent Californian. She is nineteen, very talented and exceedingly beautiful, in a black-hair-red-lips sort of way. She's been filming with Joe Yule in New Mexico and her boyfriend is – or used to be – one of the producers. She makes Lila Riley look like Dora the Explorer. If this is the sort of thing Joe Yule likes, Jenny never stood a chance.

Still she doesn't call me, or text me, or answer any of the texts I send to her.

'I knew it,' said Edie, when I tell her. 'Oh, Nonie, you're upset too. D'you want me to come over?'

We watch the ceremony together. Joe wins Best Supporting Actor. Sigrid Santorini, sitting beside him and shimmering in off-the-shoulder Givenchy, looks suitably thrilled when he gets up to accept the award. Jenny, sitting nearby in her beautiful grey Chanel, looks like a ghost. We rewind to her red carpet moment – which is gone in a flash – and she seems lost in all the pleats and feathers. She seems lost altogether. Even her hair seems to have downgraded its shade to a dull muddy orange. There's another brief image of her when *Kid Code* is nominated for Best Picture. She doesn't seem to care either way and the camera moves on.

Still no text.

We have to wait until she comes home to hear the full story. When she tells it, her voice is lifeless. It's as if she's talking about a girl she met once, a long time ago, and can't remember very well.

'It was my fault,' she says. 'You were right, Edie. All the time.'

'But he asked you to go to the ceremony with him.'

'He explained about that at the party. Sigrid was still splitting up with her boyfriend. He wasn't sure if she'd be able to come. And he knew it would look odd if he said he was coming on his own, so it was easier to say he was going with me. After all, no-one would ever imagine *we* were a couple. He knew I'd understand.'

'But you *didn't* understand,' Edie says angrily.

I can tell she's angry with Joe, not Jenny. It seems pretty clear that he quite liked having a younger girl go gooey over him when he wasn't sure what was happening with Sigrid, and he knew exactly what he was doing.

'It's not his fault,' Jenny says. It's like she's defending her father all over again. 'Anyway, it doesn't matter. I'm here. He's there.'

'But what about your new movie? The Hawaii one.'

'I'm not doing it,' she says in her empty voice. 'I was

silly to think of it. Of course I'd be awful.'

'No you wouldn't!' I say loyally.

'Well . . .' Edie is less loyal, but more honest. 'You said you wanted more practice. More training. Sounds like a good idea to me.'

Jenny nods. 'I know it's the right thing to do. I've told my agent not to look at any more movies. I'm not even sure why I've *got* an agent. I was just . . . silly. Anyway, it turns out he'd have been in Prague then anyway, so I'd have looked pretty stupid.'

'At least you'll never have to see him again,' Edie points out, searching for crumbs of comfort.

'Except at the BAFTAs, of course,' Jenny says. She half-smiles at the awfulness of it. We don't dare. 'In four weeks. They're here in London so I have to go. He's coming over with Sigrid. Because I'm such a great mate of his, he wants us to hang out together. He wants me to show her the sights.'

'*Seriously?*'

'Seriously.'

'What did you say?'

'I said yes. What else could I say? By the way, these are for you.'

She picks up a box and hands it to Edie.

'The latest Louboutins they gave me to go with the dress. Auction them for your Invisible Children.'

'Thanks.' Edie takes the box and opens it. A pair of stilettos are nestled inside, under a blanket of tissue paper. The red soles are hardly worn and the uppers sparkle with diamanté. Cinderella shoes.

'Sure you don't want to keep them?'

'What do you think?'

'I'll make sure they go to a good home.'

Chapter 34

*W*hen Jenny goes, Edie hangs around. I can tell she wants to talk to me about something, but I have to ask what it is.

'I was wondering . . .' she says, '. . . would it be a good idea to name the school after Henry Lamogi? The one we're trying to build? I was thinking about the Henry Lamogi Memorial School, but I wasn't sure. I know I put my foot in it sometimes.'

'*Do* you?'

'You know I do.'

'I meant did you *know*. But it sounds like a nice idea. If Crow agrees, of course. No-one's told her yet, though, have they?'

Edie shakes her head.

'No. But Andy Elat has offered to fly the family over for the show. He wants them to see what she can do. And he wants Crow to be able to see Victoria again. She hasn't seen her since she was a baby. So James can tell her . . . you know . . . in person, about Henry. But don't tell her about them coming. Andy wants it to be a surprise.'

I promise secrecy. I'm getting used to it.

The thought of James coming over gives me a shred of hope for Crow.

'So does that mean there's a chance her dad'll let her stay?'

Edie shakes her head again.

'Not really. Not from what he's said.'

'But surely it helps that she's got us? Looking after her?'

Edie looks embarrassed. 'Well, not exactly. People have been telling him about my blog. I'm afraid he thinks you're a bad influence.'

'Why?'

She gestures at me. I look down. Today I haven't got any scary meetings so I'm in lederhosen, customised wellies and a frilly shirt. Gradually it dawns on me.

'You mean he disapproves of me because of my *outfits*?'

She looks embarrassed.

'That's all he knows about you. That, and the fact you keep introducing Crow to people who "distract her with their superficial affectations".'

'Great. Thanks.'

Edie sees the look I give her and goes the colour of the tee-shirts. She also manages to remember something else so she can change the subject, quickly.

'They don't want front row seats, by the way. They want it to be a surprise, but they don't want to give Crow a heart attack. They want to stand near the back somewhere.'

Small mercies. If that's the case, they'll be about the only people in London who do.

Chapter 35

*C*row may not be news in the celebrity press, but she's news in the fashion press. It's divided between the people who think she may be the next Galliano, and the people who assume she's just a jumped-up little teenager with good connections, who's bound to fall flat on her face when the collection turns out to be a disaster. For these reasons, both groups of people badly want tickets for the show. I get calls and emails all the time from people 'just checking' they're on the list. I don't have the heart to tell most of them they haven't got a hope.

With less than six weeks to go, the mood board in the Battersea studio is starting to look ready. We've decided on the gold eyeshadow and dusty gold and silver blusher for the models. We've got a good idea of the soft, romantic ringlets for the hair. Skye has found someone to make the tiara-like headdresses Crow wants. We've even chosen the tights.

All the *toiles* have been made and several of the dresses are starting to come together. Crow's designed the invitations. And the Year Ten art class at school are making the backdrop saying 'Less Fashion More Compassion'. I hope the visiting fashionistas will find it ironic, rather than positively offensive, but it's too late now.

The studio is beautiful. It's become the story of the Twelve Dancing Princesses – full of jewel-coloured silks, frayed fabrics, scattered crystals and tired helpers. However, it's also a crazy mess. There's still loads to do and we have to fit it around maths, English and French, same as always.

In the centre is the *pièce de résistance*. It's the showstopper dress that Crow's going to use to wind up the show. Lots of designers end with a wedding dress, but as Crow's theme is dancing princesses, this is just the most perfect party dress, for the most perfect girl.

Unlike the rest of the collection, which is intensely coloured, this dress is silver. It's got a backless satin bodice and a long, waterfall skirt made up of dozens of petals of silver lace, finished with crystals. The lace is Skye's latest textile design, which she's given to Crow to experiment with. It's even more delicate than her last one and looks like the skeletons of leaves you get on a frosty winter morning. It seems incredibly delicate, but Crow has decided to muck about with it and fray the edges of every petal. Each one takes hours of work, deciding on the shape and position and then fraying it the perfect amount.

The effect isn't as ballerina-pretty as most of her stuff. It's more edgy and sexy and dangerous. It takes me a while to work out what on earth can be going on in that thirteen-year-old head of hers to make her even imagine it, until I realise: it's like a crash-course in fashion history. There are bits of Vionnet, bits of Saint Laurent, bits of Westwood, bits of Galliano and bits that are entirely her own.

One day, she catches me looking.

'I call it the Swan,' she says. 'It sort of started out as a design for *Swan Lake*. One day I'd love to design for the ballet.'

Of course she would. Really, nothing surprises me about Crow any more. She probably will, knowing her.

Chapter 36

*J*anuary hurtles into February. I actually feel sick when Mum turns the page on the kitchen calendar. February is Fashion Week month. February is like a magical name for something in the future that will never really happen. Once February comes we only have three weeks to get everything done. Lots of my friends are thinking about skiing. I'm thinking about lighting and rehearsals and the dreaded seating plan.

Most Sunday evenings are spent making props, or working on the music with Harry, or desperately finishing homework. My ability to précis, I'm told, has much improved. This means I've got good at making my essays short. A necessity in these busy times.

The second Sunday in February is an exception, though.

It's BAFTA Sunday and work at the studio has ground to a halt. Edie and I are outside the Royal Opera House in Covent Garden. For once, Crow is with us too, looking scared and startled. I don't think she likes big crowds and this is the biggest crowd I've been in, and the most excited.

Jenny had been hoping to arrive late and avoid the red carpet as much as possible, but the message obviously hasn't got through and she's one of the first people to turn up. This time she gets a warm welcome as lots of people recognise her. There are a few friendly shouts as people hold up their phones to get a picture. I try too, but all I get is a picture of a field of mobiles. However, from a distance, she seems to be bearing up well.

Mum would approve. Crow has somehow found the time to design an emerald green satin dress with a tiny waist and what we now call a Jenny-length hem that shows off her calves and ankles. The student helpers have mostly put it together, because Crow is so busy finalising the collection she hardly sleeps as it is, and they've managed to embellish the bodice and hem with some leftover Swarovski crystals. There's a matching jacket, too, to ward off the freezing English night.

The original Louboutins look good with their new rose clips. Jenny's also wearing borrowed emerald earrings and a choker with a teeny emerald drop, to emphasise the perfect skin on her neck and shoulders. Granny's hairdresser has conditioned her hair to such a shine it's practically blinding.

The only thing we can't really help her with is her expression. That will be entirely down to acting.

Joe arrives not long after Jenny, clutching Sigrid Santorini's hand and looking sickeningly pleased with himself. Sigrid is beautiful in pictures and better in the flesh. She has perfect hair, perfect tan, perfect body, and has encased it tonight in a gold lamé dress that starts at mid-boob level and stops a couple of inches above her perfect knees. She must be freezing but she's too professional to show it. Both of them show perfect sets of not entirely natural white teeth to us and all the photographers.

Jenny stays where she is, signing autographs, looking serene and unconcerned. Just another girl Joe happens to know from a movie. Because they were in *Kid Code* together the photographers ask them to pose beside each other and they do. Despite everything, they look as good as they did the last time. Joe mutters something into Jenny's ear and she smiles, as if her heart isn't really broken.

Edie and I agree that if she'd performed this well during *Kid Code* she'd be one of the favourites for an award tonight.

This time, she calls as soon as she gets home.

'Thank God that's over.'

I tell her how good she was on the red carpet and ask if they won anything.

'Four,' she says abruptly. She reels off what they were, but it's as if she's listing GCSE subjects. There's clearly something else on her mind.

'Can you do me a favour?' she asks.

'Sure.'

'It's about Sigrid. You know we were going to do things together? Well, Joe's got to go to this business thing tomorrow and Sigrid's stuck on her own. She was busy admiring my dress, so I told her we could go to Crow's studio, if she wanted. She loves the whole Fashion Week thing. She often goes to shows in New York, she says. And Paris. She gets tickets all the time.'

'It'll be chaos!' I say, appalled. 'There's stuff every-where and pieces being finished off. She can't go!'

'She'll have to,' Jenny says, sounding tearful. 'I prom-ised.'

I sigh deeply. I can't bear to hear her sounding this miserable. I'll have to go with her, though, to guide the starlet through the pandemonium. With the show looming, the place is littered with nearly finished pieces, boxes of trimmings, discarded fabrics, stray accessories and piles of paperwork. It's impossible to imagine it all being ready on time but luckily I have Amanda's reassur-ance that this is normal and somehow, it will all come together when it needs to.

'When were you thinking of going?'

'Six o'clock? After school?'

Well, at six on a Monday I'd normally be at the studio anyway, so I agree.

This Monday, I'm there at five to. Unusually, no-one else

is, but I hope this means the others are getting some rest for a change. The place is empty and dark. I haven't seen it like this for weeks. It feels strange to turn the lights on and gradually watch the pieces appear from the darkness as each strip light flickers into life.

I'm used to the chaos, but behind me, I hear a gasp. I look round and see Sigrid in the doorway, smiling like a toothpaste ad, with Jenny hovering behind her.

Sigrid's wearing a jeans and cashmere jumper combo that manages to look casual and eye-poppingly expensive. Her handbag is gorgeous, if you like that sort of thing. Her hair is shiny. Her skin is dewy. Her tiny, perfectly proportioned body doesn't have a square inch of fat on it. She is bouncy and friendly and gives the impression that she has just downed four energy drinks and loves you to bits. I don't think she's noticed I hate her.

Jenny's wearing an old coat and an apologetic expression. She introduces me.

'Er, welcome. It's not always this messy,' I say, lying.

'Oh no! It's fabulous. Awesome,' says Sigrid, going up to one of the tailor's dummies and ruffling its feathery skirt. 'Jenny, I totally love this stuff. Where's your little friend?'

Jenny shrugs and looks at me questioningly. I shrug back.

'Nonie's in charge, though,' Jenny explains to reassure Sigrid. 'She's the brains behind the business.'

I haven't heard myself described this way before and I

don't think brains behind businesses usually giggle. But Sigrid ignores me and wafts around between the dummies, running her hand over the fabrics and feeling the petals and the crystal embroidery. Everything is 'neat' and 'awesome'. I pray she doesn't break anything, but it seems rude to ask her not to touch.

'Would you like a cup of tea?' I ask, feeling a bit desperate and anxious to give her hands something else to do.

'Warm water, please,' says Sigrid decisively. 'With a touch of lemon. Three drops. Fresh lemon, please. You are SO sweet.'

They really are like that. Some of them, anyway. You think they're going to surprise you and be vaguely normal, but no.

I look at the studio's kitchenette, with its kettle, sink and mini-fridge. In the end I give her warmish tap water without the lemon. She takes one sip and hands it to Jenny with a wave of her hand. Then she continues on her royal progress round the room. Some of the stuff isn't awesome or neat, it's cute.

Eventually she reaches the showpiece of the collection – the Swan. It's the only piece that's technically ready, although even now Crow adjusts it every time she sees it.

'Oh,' Sigrid gasps again. She stops dead. 'Jeez, this is the one. This has to be the one. I have to do this award thing. Can I try it on? How much are these numbers?'

My brain feels as though it's been chucked over a cliff

and is bouncing down the boulders. Award thing. Try on. How much. I haven't really pictured actually selling the items after the show – although of course that's the point. Certainly not to an A-lister like Sigrid. Crow would take it in her stride, I'm sure. But she's not here.

I'm so busy stuttering, working out what to think, that Sigrid's got the dress off the dummy before I can stop her.

'Help me here,' she says, heading over to the mirror.

Then she casually strips to her knickers and steps into the dress. She's a minuscule sample size, naturally, and it fits her like a glove. It looks as though it was made for her. It looks as though it was made ON her. I can't help gasping, which is obviously the effect she was looking for. I haven't seen it on a moving human being before and it's incredible. It's a living fairy-tale of a dress and Sigrid, star-stealing strumpet that she is, looks incredible in it.

She stands in front of the mirror for several minutes, preening and practising her poses on tiptoe. It looks gorgeous from every angle. Not a single seam needs adjusting.

'Awesome,' she says for the umpteenth time. 'Can I take it?'

'I'm afraid not,' I explain. 'London Fashion Week starts in just over a week. We need it for fittings and stuff. Then the show, of course.'

'Cute,' Sigrid says dismissively. 'When's the show?'

'In twelve days,' I say, holding out my hands to help her out of the dress. She doesn't move.

'That's OK. My award thing'll be over by then. It's just SO gorgeous. I have to have it. And I'm leaving town tomorrow.' She looks thoughtful. 'There wouldn't be time for you to ship it. Safest if I take it with me.'

'I'm really sorry, but we need it.'

Sigrid looks at me, round-eyed. 'Of course you do. I promise I'll get it back to you in a couple days. A week, tops. Scout's honour. Isn't that what you say? And meanwhile I'll wear it on TV and you'll get all the coverage. Think what that'll mean to your little friend here. She'll love you for it.'

I'm not quite sure what happens next. Jenny seems to have dematerialised. Sigrid says more stuff and I keep saying sorry, no, and she gets out of the dress and back into her cashmere, and the next thing I know she's got the Swan in a bag and her taxi is waiting to take her back to her hotel and we're outside the studio and I'm waving her goodbye.

It's only as the taxi pulls away that I start to wake up.

'Why didn't you take it off her?' Jenny asks.

It turns out Jenny disappeared to the loo at the crucial moment. Now she's standing beside me, watching the taxi drive off.

'Why didn't *you*?'

'Dunno. I was sort of mesmerised. She does that. But anyway, I thought you'd given it to her. You did, didn't you?'

'I suppose I did,' I admit. 'She promised she'd get it

back to us in time.'

'When did she say she was going to wear it exactly?'

'This award thing she's got.'

'Which award thing?'

I look at Jenny, panicking.

'I don't know. Some award thing. Isn't there a big award thing in a couple of days or so?'

Jenny shrugs. Her award thing days are over.

'There's only the Oscars that I know of. But they're not for two weeks. And anyway, Sigrid's already got her outfit sorted for that. She was telling me. Going on about it, quite a lot. It's the three Vs.'

I cut her off. I'm not listening any more. My skin's gone cold. It'll be all right, I tell myself. It'll be completely fine. There's a perfectly rational explanation. Worst case, we just call her and ask for it back.

Over the next three hours, various things happen.

Sigrid isn't taking calls. We establish that her flight is at dawn.

When we get home we google – and can't find – any 'award thing' that she might be attending in any major world city in the next couple of days. And if she doesn't send the dress back after that it risks being too late for the show. Which doesn't bear thinking about.

Crow arrives to pick up a notebook and I have to tell her that I have GIVEN HER DRESS AWAY to a girl she's never met, and whom we don't even like.

I have to listen to Mum saying how she simply can't believe how stupid I am. And watch Harry's dumbstruck expression, which is worse.

Amanda Elat calls out of the blue just to check that everything's OK and I have to watch Crow's face as she explains that the Swan is gone. This is worst of all.

Edie comes round and says I look like Jenny did the night of the *Kid Code* dinner, when Joe first went public with Sigrid. I feel sick.

I am sick.

Between them, Edie, Jenny and Mum put me to bed.

It's only as they're putting my light out that I realise I've been in such shock I haven't even apologised to Crow.

Chapter 37

I've never seen Crow lost for ideas before when it comes to designing. Up to now, whatever's happened, whatever's been thrown at her, she's just been able to put pen to paper and run up a fabulous little number, problem sorted.

But not this time.

The Swan summed up all the inspiration and all the skill she'd gained over the last two years. It was what the whole collection had been building up to.

And it's not as if we can just run up another one. The Swan took hundreds of hours to make. It also used up most of the small stock of silver lace that Skye made by hand.

Listlessly, more for something to do than anything else, I call Skye. It turns out she's just sold the last of the fabric to a designer in Milan. Mum calls Milan for me. They say yes, they've got the fabric and we can have it by courier if we absolutely need it.

For five hundred pounds. Plus shipping.

So that's that.

On Tuesday, as soon as Jenny sees me at school, she yells at me.

'I've found it!'

'The Swan?'

She nods. I practically crumple at the good news.

'Well, I know where it's going to be. I googled and googled. In the end I texted Joe. Sigrid's going to collect an award from the Spanish film industry on Saturday. That's the award thingy.'

'But she's only been in one movie!'

'One big one. Loads of little independent ones, apparently. But that big one made a lot of money.'

'You said Saturday?'

I'm busy doing mental calculations. Wear dress. Get home – well, back to hotel room, anyway. Give dress to stylist to ship back to London. Put dress on plane (who will pay for that?). If we're super-lucky, we could get the Swan back on Monday or Tuesday next week, which might be in time for model fittings and rehearsals for the show on Friday.

Assuming Sigrid is efficient. And considerate.

'It'll be OK,' Jenny reassures me.

I leave yet another message on Sigrid's assistant's mobile, wishing her luck on Saturday and reminding her about the dress. No answer.

The next evening Harry comes in late from college with a big grin on his face.

Everyone has heard about my crazy giveaway by now, and family know not to talk loudly, smile or look in any way cheerful in my presence. I glare at him.

'Problem solved,' he says. 'How much do you need?'

'Thousands of pounds,' I snort grumpily. 'Five hundred for fabric. And shipping. And we need to pay professionals to help out with the sewing because otherwise it just can't be done in time. At professional rates. I always thought couture dresses were expensive for what they were, but they're positively cheap.'

We've decided not to ask Andy Elat and Amanda for any more money. And they haven't offered any. I get the impression they're leaving me to sort this one out on my own.

'Will fifteen hundred do?' Harry asks.

'It would help,' I say with a hollow cackle.

'Here,' he says. He puts an envelope on the table. In it are more twenty-pound notes than I've ever seen in my life.

What's he done? Started dealing drugs?

I look at him suspiciously. So does Mum.

'I sold my camera,' he says.

This seems odd. His snappy camera's very nice, but it's probably worth about two of these notes, and the only other ones he's got are proper ones for college.

'Which camera?' Mum asks in a strained sort of way.

'The Leica. And the lens.'

Mum and I both stare at him.

'The blurry lens? But that was a present from your dad!' I say.

'But you need that for your degree!' Mum groans.

'Oh, thanks, Harry. That was a good idea of yours. I'm so grateful,' he says with cheerful sarcasm. 'I sold them to a guy on the course. He's always liked them. I think I may switch from photography next term anyway. I'm wondering if I'm more of a painter after all.'

Mum buries her head in her hands.

'Wow, thanks,' I say at last. 'That was a good idea of yours. I'm so grateful.'

'Go buy lace,' he says. 'With my blessing.'

Chapter 38

It's Sunday. I'm googling the Spanish film institute presentation, looking for images of the stars getting their awards yesterday. It's not the easiest thing in the world to find, but eventually I track down a couple of pictures.

Hot Spanish male star, check. Hot Spanish female star, check. Then, finally, a picture of Sigrid and Joe looking practically glued together and manically happy.

She's in a little black number. By Rodarte, apparently. Very pretty. Totally appropriate. She looks great.

No sign of the Swan.

Her assistant still isn't returning my calls. Joe isn't returning Jenny's.

Meanwhile, life goes on. Crow's studio is starting to look more organised. Finished pieces are draped with dust covers. The walls are splattered with Polaroids of me and Edie in the various outfits (looking pretty silly) to give an idea of how it will all fit together. We're all wearing our pink tee-shirts. There is a wall of invitations to fashion parties we'll be too busy to attend. And some we can't resist. Goodie bags are stacked in a corner, full of nice things from Miss Teen and updates from Edie on the Invisible Children campaign and the plans for the (Henry Lamogi Memorial) school for Victoria and her friends.

The new show-stopper dress isn't here. It's being worked on by someone Yvette has found for us who is even quicker at sewing than Crow. However, the design for it is on the wall. Harry's christened it 'Swan-Lite'. It's a mini version of the original (not enough time or fabric to recreate the full waterfall skirt), with a bit less boning and draping, but still giving the general idea. It will be beautiful. Everyone is very careful not to talk about it in front of me. Which of course makes me feel terrible.

I have my laptop open in a corner. I'm trying to complete a history project and sort out shoe deliveries by email when my mobile rings. I very nearly don't answer it, because while I can handle doing two things at once, three might be pushing it. However, when I hear Svetlana's giggly Russian tones down the line, I instantly forget history AND shoes.

'Is it true your brother sold his camera to help Crow finish the collection?' she asks.

'How on earth do you know?' I know the fashion world is small, but this is ridiculous. It's New York Fashion Week at the moment and Svetlana must be on the other side of the Atlantic (or is it the Pacific?), busily rushing from show to show. She's bound to be in most of them.

'Skye told me,' she says. 'Your brother is such a cutie. Tell him I'm still listening to that playlist he did for me. Why didn't he call me?'

'He tried,' I tell her. 'But you were always on planes.'

'So? I'm *always* on planes. Guys can't take it personally. It drives me crazy. He just has to try a bit harder.'

'I'll let him know,' I assure her.

'Good. What was I going to say? Oh yes. Would Crow like me to walk for her, do you think? It sounds as if you could do with a bit of help. I can fit it in if I'm rude to a lot of very important people and miss an unmissable party.' More giggles.

'Well, actually, we're kind of OK for models,' I say.

She must know I'm joking. Luckily, she does.

'Cool. I'll let you know when I'm back in town. See you.'

I look at my mobile, convinced I've just dreamt the whole thing. I even shake it.

'Who was that?' Crow asks.

'Svetlana.'

'Oh, that's nice. Is she OK?'

'Fine. Actually . . . she'd like to model for you.'

Crow gives me a relaxed, cheerful smile.

'Oh good.'

She goes back to finishing the bodice she's working

233

on. In Crow's world, it's perfectly natural for a SUPER-MODEL to OFFER to work for you. Now I'm certain I must be dreaming.

Back at home, I try the news on Harry over supper.

I try to be as casual as I can.

'Er, just thought you'd like to know. Svetlana sends her love. And she liked the thing about your camera. And she's going to model for Crow, so I guess you'll see her then. While you're DJ-ing. She said to call.'

'Oh, OK then.'

For a minute he has me, but then he drops his knife and fork, bursts out laughing, leans over and gives me such a bear-hug it squeezes the breath out of me.

Mum comes out with another couple of words from my Converses.

Which is reassuring, because I was starting to think I'd entered some sort of parallel universe where this sort of thing was normal.

Chapter 39

It's the twentieth of February. Mum's ringed it in red on the calendar. Today's the day.

I'm standing opposite a photographer's gallery just off Bond Street. Watching the scrum.

Mum's photography friend has lent us the space and we've turned it into a mad artist's Parisian studio based on my dad's – not that he's mad or anything. Actually, he's in the audience. We spent the whole of last night talking about the show when he came over and we hardly got any sleep. Dad's brilliant that way. He says you can always sleep when you're older. And he's wangled loads of invitations to fashion parties while he's here. And he says I've grown up so much he can't really call me his little cabbage any more. But he does anyway, luckily.

He went into the gallery hours ago. Normally you'd hardly notice the place, but right now it's impossible to miss because it's surrounded by a heaving mass of women in high heels and Louis Vuitton scarves and clothes you can't buy in shops yet, all desperate for a decent seat and waving their BlackBerries and shouting out that I've personally said they can be in the front row. I said it was a nightmare.

Fortunately, there's security on the door. Amanda said we'd need it, particularly after Svetlana announced she was modelling. I've got my arms full of coffees and muffins (models need loads of energy and we massively under-ordered). In order to get back in, I have to get through the scrum so I duck my head down, flash my pass, and leave them to it.

Inside, seven leggy, exquisite models are being turned into golden dancing princesses, with tumbling hair and glittering skin. At the fittings, they all looked pale, jet-lagged and emaciated. This morning, after a bit of hair and makeup, they look like goddesses. Goddesses listening to their iPods, or scoffing muffins, or catching up on a bestseller, but goddesses nevertheless.

I check the rails. Eight models. Twelve outfits. Fifty pieces. Six minutes. I can do this. If I concentrate hard enough, I think I can do this.

Jenny's become a hairdresser's assistant, dressed in her 'Less Fashion More Compassion' tee-shirt and – finally – some cropped jeans that look Marilyn-fabulous on her. She teases me that I have, after all, pretty much ended up making the tea, but I simply poke my tongue out at her. I am VERY IMPORTANT today and everyone needs my opinion on stuff.

Granny's hairdresser has agreed to work for us as a favour. Everyone looks gorgeous. Even the models seem to have more cheekbones after he's finished with them. I realise that my problem is not my face, it's my HAIR. If only I'd discovered this years ago.

Through the doorway, I can hear Harry's sound check in the main gallery. Snatches of Tchaikovsky and Ella Fitzgerald, David Bowie and Chopin. It's very eclectic, but it makes sense to us. The models are tapping their elegant feet. Fingers crossed.

Crow looks like a taller version of the girl I first saw sketching the court dress in the V&A. Same serious expression. Same faraway look in her eyes. Today she's in home-made black satin dungarees. It's the models who'll be wearing the interesting stuff. She's talking to the producer we've hired (at vast expense – bye bye budget), who'll be ensuring the show runs like clockwork. Unlike DJ Rémi, he doesn't seem to mind working with infants and he seems to be having a good time.

Svetlana isn't here yet. She told us she might be late. She's finishing off another show and she's got a taxi booked to get here pronto, so there's nothing we can do except wait.

Before security let the scrum through, Amanda and I make last-minute changes to the seating, to reflect the INCREASINGLY IMPORTANT people who've managed to beg, borrow or steal invitations to the show.

Skye is chief wardrobe mistress. She's dyed her hair to

match the precise pink of her tee-shirt. Mum is our makeup maestro. She and her tee-shirt are covered in stray gold glitter. It suits her. She grins when I come back to check on everyone. Recently she's been turning her BlackBerry off a lot so she can talk to me about how things are going. And confiding that she's seriously wondering if Harry will ever graduate from St Martins. It's as if she's suddenly noticed me. Which is really nice. And she's been positively complimentary about my cobweb-sleeve mini-dress. I almost miss the snarky comments.

Gradually, the gallery fills with eager fashionistas, all busy talking about what they did last night, how hungry they are and which parties they're going to later.

Granny's making do with her second-row seat and leaning forward to have an animated conversation with the editor of a national magazine. From Japan. Florence and Yvette, beside her, look simply happy to be here. Dad is a few seats away, looking like a man who badly needs a Gitane. Edie slips in at the back and gets someone to let me know that our most important guests have arrived.

Still no Svetlana. We're starting to run out of champagne. I wonder how long the fashionistas will be prepared to wait, but they seem used to it.

Then suddenly there's a sort of ruffle in the air, like a breeze blowing through, and I realise something big must have happened. Svetlana arrives and throws her coat off, into the arms of her waiting dresser.

Mum comes out with a couple of French swear-words that didn't even make it on to the Converses. I look over. The show was due to start ten minutes ago and Svetlana is covered in blue foundation. From head to toe. Even her hair is blue.

'I know!' she says, stripping casually to her knickers. 'Nightmare. It was a sort of space-alien show. I tried to warn you.'

She had tried to warn us. Yesterday. But what she meant by 'a bit of blue makeup' and what we thought she meant were two different things. Mum gets to work on her with industrial quantities of Nivea and makeup remover, while I go and warn Harry that he's going to have to keep the crowd entertained for a while.

Eventually, only fifty minutes late, Svetlana is looking as goddess-like as the rest of them. Possibly more so. Harry pauses the music. The anxious rustling from the audience dies down a bit. The photographers run off a few practice shots. It's time to start.

For a moment, the only sound is my heart beating VERY LOUDLY. I'm sure they can hear it at the back. Then Harry kicks off with Ella singing jazz. Six minutes. That's all the time Crow has to show the fashion world what she's made of, and what her dreams are. In six minutes it will be over.

I'm wearing a headset so the producer can tell me when to send the models down the catwalk. He gives me the signal.

'Romance,' I whisper.

The first model sashays onto the catwalk. Her dress is garnet-red, short, petal skirt swaying. Her headdress twinkles in her hair. Behind me, Crow is busy adjusting skirts and arranging sleeves. Mum and Granny's hairdresser are poised beside me, ready to make last-minute tweaks. The models seem to ignore us. They're thinking about the choreography, not falling over, and projecting the look.

I suppose it must be six minutes, but what happens next feels like six totally fabulous, totally action-packed hours. Or possibly days. Each outfit is a beautiful story. The music carries the models along. The bank of photographers provides a light show all of its own. Behind the scenes, we all rush about like mad things. As each model comes off, she sticks her arms up in the air and her dresser gets busy, whipping clothes off, whipping them on; everyone's adjusting hair, retouching makeup, gesticulating frantically at me, desperately trying to ensure that we don't send one of the goddesses out in her bra.

Beyond the catwalk, I can hear lots of whirring and popping from photographers' cameras over the sound of Harry's music, but I haven't got time to worry about what the audience are thinking. I'm just checking that we're doing justice to Crow's outfits. So far so good. At least nobody's collapsed on the catwalk.

And then suddenly Svetlana is standing in front of me

in the Swan-Lite, looking magnificent. It's almost possible to imagine that Crow deliberately designed it this short to show off her truly incredible legs. She stoops to give Crow a quick gold-powder kiss and then she's off down the catwalk. And we can hear something else over Harry's David Bowie finale.

It sounds like raindrops on a tin roof.

It's clapping.

They're standing and clapping. All of them. Granny and Yvette and Florence and the Japanese editor and TWO of my favourite designers and three It-girls and as many PRs as you can humanly fit in the space. And they really love it. This isn't just 'Didn't the kid from Africa do a nice job after all?' clapping, this is 'Wow – seriously wow!' clapping.

The other models come back in to join Svetlana and there is a general call for Crow, but at first no joy. I knew this would happen. Her delight was in dreaming up these outfits, not showing off beside them. However, I've planned for this eventuality. I practically carry her on to the catwalk and the models grab at her hands, pulling her forward, forcing her to stand there and take her bow.

I lurk behind everyone, peering into the blackness near the back. At last I spot Edie. I can see that beside her are the faces from the photographs, looking older, but as elegant as ever: James and Grace Lamogi. Crow, I realise, is the image of her father. He's standing stock still, not smiling, not clapping, but I know his daughter well enough to understand that he's drinking in every moment and I have a feeling he might be verging on a tingle of pride.

I watch Crow's shoulders in front of me. They are hunched in shy, embarrassed 'aw shucks' acknowledge-ment of the standing ovation. Then I see them straighten and stiffen. Suddenly her whole body is rigid. She's staring out across the audience and I assume she's spotted her parents. I look again and then I notice what she has seen.

James and Grace Lamogi are not alone. There's another figure standing next to them. He's staring intently at Crow, as if nothing in the world will ever break the connection. He's wearing a satchel just like the one Crow has always worn. He isn't smiling either. He's asking Crow something with his eyes.

Suddenly she leaps off the catwalk and flies across the room. How she gets there, across the seats and bodies and photographers' cameras and equipment, I'll never know. But it takes her seconds. She reaches Henry and I can hear her shriek above the rest of the commotion in the room, which is deafening.

She throws her arms around him and hugs him to her with five years' worth of hugs. Whatever it was he was asking her with his eyes, her answer is yes. Their faces are streaked with tears.

At this moment, the catwalk lights go down and are

reduced to a single spot, shining on the place where Crow was standing. The audience goes quiet. Perfect timing. NOT. There are calls throughout the audience for Crow to come back on stage. But I know she won't. We are just a background now. She's found her brother. Someone else will have to round off the show.

I step round Svetlana and into the spotlight. Strangely, my feeling of terror has gone. I think what I'm feeling is euphoria. It's like drugs, but without the rehab. Whatever it is, it makes what I'm about to do feel pretty easy.

'Thank you all for coming,' I say. Lots of cheers. I make sure I thank Skye and all the models and all our helpers and Andy and Amanda. Yup, turns out I could be good at this.

'Some of you may know,' I finish, 'that Crow has been waiting for her big brother to come home for some time. Big brothers are important people . . .' I suddenly remember Harry and give him a huge wave. He grins and waves back. 'Look in your goodie bags. Go to the website. Pledge some money. Sign the petition. Tell everybody about the Invisible Children so they can all go home.'

There's a final wave of clapping as people start reaching for their programmes and goodie bags and scraping their chairs. Then the door is opened and Edie makes sure that Crow and Henry and her family are the first to disappear. Which leaves me hanging around for the next two hours answering questions, making sure the clothes are put away safely, thanking the models again, being air-kissed a lot by excited fashion people, accepting flowers, giving directions to the after-show party, making decisions and generally doing my job.

Chapter 40

When Andy Elat puts up favoured guests in London, he doesn't do it at the nearest airport hotel. Oh no. He does it at his favourite suite at the Dorchester, popular with rock gods and movie stars. The Lamogis have it for a few days. Hollywood's Hottest Couple are due in a fortnight.

We're in the suite admiring the décor. Actually, we're not. We're bitching about the décor, which is too Art Deco for us minimalist London types and too grand for the Lamogis.

It's Sunday. Tonight, we're here to watch the Oscars on one of the suite's massive, oversize TVs. *Kid Code* is up for three and despite the fact that Joe-we-hate-him-Yule is nominated for one of them, Jenny is so excited she doesn't know what to do with herself.

The producers invited her to LA for all the parties and hoopla, but she couldn't face it. The prospect of spending several days trying to avoid Joe and Sigrid was her idea of hell, but she still wanted to experience the thing vicariously, from thousands of miles away. We, of course, are happy to keep her company. Oscars are fashion heaven. I require no encouragement to be glued to the screen.

Crow is sitting on Henry's lap, looking more like a little girl past her bedtime than a fashion queen. Edie, Jenny and I are cross-legged on the floor, eating Phish Food ice cream, drinking hot chocolate and feeling slightly queasy. Little Victoria is snuggled up beside me, wrapped in a blanket. Harry refuses to sully the temple that is his rock-god body with our chocolate delights. He's sullying it with beer instead, along with Crow's dad and Henry. The mothers are contenting themselves with champagne.

There's an awful lot of waffle around the Oscars. Never have so many irrelevant fashion facts been quoted by so many journalists about so few stars. And it goes on for hours. I absolutely love it. So do Jenny and Crow.

The stars start to arrive and the red-carpet presenters get out amongst them, asking questions about what they're wearing, or rather, 'who' they're wearing, and gushing about the weirdest outfits. The theme this year seems to be big skirts and tiny waists. Everybody has one or the other or both, if they're girls, and if they're blokes they show up with a girl who's got them and try not to tread on her hem.

Hollywood's Hottest Female is one exception, but in a

good way. I expect we'll see her in all the magazines next week. She's gone for a vintage Saint Laurent tuxedo and trousers, which look completely fabulous on her and get her twenty trillion fashion points for being slightly daring and honouring the great man's passing. (She doesn't look as good as Svetlana did in the Battersea marquee, but only us fashion insiders know that.) She's in serious contention for the Best Actress Oscar, given that she's up for *Kid Code* and an arthouse movie she released in December, so she gets a lot of attention. In simple lines and black and white, she stands out against the crowd. Her husband just looks his usual gorgeous self.

We give the other stars points. Natalie Portman gets loads. Meryl Streep not so many. Angelina Jolie's earrings are so beautiful it hurts. Mum wants them. I want them. Even Grace Lamogi can't help sighing at the thought of them.

Then Jenny spots Joe Yule on the red carpet. I watch her carefully. She's very, very still, but she doesn't look as ghostly as she did a month ago. I think she's getting over it. I turn back to the screen. For a moment, I'm distracted by the green lasers. Then I suddenly realise what's coming next. I'm the one to look ghostly this time. I catch my breath and hold it. The whole room is completely silent.

Where is she? What has she chosen? Jenny said it was the three 'V's. Eventually I asked her what they were and she said: vintage, Versace or Valentino. We can't bear it. Edie clutches my arm and the skin around her fingers goes white.

The camera pans to Sigrid. And there she is.

Glimmering silver. I think it's Valentino. My vision's gone blurry and I can't concentrate.

Out of the corner of my eye I can just about make out Jenny jumping up and down and hyperventilating.

'It is, it is, it IS!'

Everyone turns to look at me. Gradually, it starts to sink in. I'm looking at Sigrid's perfectly toned back above a frayed and layered waterfall skirt. Then she turns and the light catches the shimmering satin of the bustier. She's worn it with diamanté sandals and a rope of diamonds. As you do.

She chose the Swan. Over vintage, Versace and Valentino. Oh. My. God.

'Hey, look. Over THERE,' says Female Presenter. 'Sigrid! Sigrid! Come over here, gorgeous. You're looking WONDERFUL.'

Sigrid comes over for a quick interview and about a billion people see the dress. Edie's fingers are still biting into me.

'Who are you WEARING? I've never seen anything like it. It's INCREDIBLE.'

Sigrid may not be my favourite movie star, but she's a perfect clothes horse and she knows what to do on the red carpet. She twists and poses and shows the dress from every angle.

'This is by a young designer in London called Crow.

It's from her first collection.'

She flashes a smile that I feel is aimed straight at me. A sort of triumphant apology. 'A week tops', my foot. No wonder she's been avoiding me. She's had that dress a fortnight by now and it feels like a year.

'My! I'm LIKING the LOOK,' Female Presenter pronounces. 'Who did you say? Crow? FABULOUS, darling. You're the belle of the ball.'

Sigrid turns to waft up the red carpet. Jenny whacks me on the back.

I haven't breathed yet and apparently I've gone slightly blue.

Chapter 41

$\mathcal{I}$t's September. We're standing in the costume section of the V&A. I'm beside Crow, who's wearing painted silk dungarees and a tee-shirt that was a present from Stella McCartney. I'm in a vintage Balenciaga cocktail dress that Granny has finally let me borrow. It looked much too old on me until I customised it with some felt flowers and teamed it with my tartan tights and Converses. Now I think it will just about do.

We're staring at a new case that's just been set up near the steps leading down towards the café. Out of the corner of my eye, I can see Vivienne Westwood, whom Mum's just introduced me to. She said (Mum, not Vivienne) that I was the person who made all of this happen and she's totally, totally proud of me. I'm so glad I'm not wearing mascara yet. It would be all down the Balenciaga.

Vivienne said something, but my brain was going 'La la la la Dame Vivienne Westwood is talking to you la la la,' so I'll have to ask Mum later what it was. I think it might have been how much she enjoyed Crow's show, although I'm pretty sure she wasn't there. Too busy with her own. Maybe she's seen a video. It's a total hit on YouTube. I think I'm responsible for half the views, though.

Crow's looking critically at the case and I can tell she's doing some mental redesign, but it's too late now. Inside is the Swan, fitted onto a mannequin that bears more than a passing resemblance to Sigrid Santorini. The V&A asked for it after all the hoopla over Crow's show and the Oscars. We paid for shipping and Sigrid sent it back to us, along with a glossy photo of herself wearing it on the night, which is in the case too. At least she had the decency to get it cleaned. The curator has stood the mannequin on a red carpet and put fake movie lights all round the case so there's more than a hint of Oscar about the thing.

After the Sigrid red-carpet appearance, our phones didn't stop ringing for weeks. We had to hire people to answer them in the end, so we could find the time to go to school. Although Crow has moved away from the Three Bitches. James Lamogi has bowed to the inevitable and agreed to let his daughter stay in London, but not at that school. Edie's mum has found another one that's really good for children with dyslexia. And they're pretty good at giving her time off to design dresses for TOP HOLLYWOOD ACTRESSES to wear on GLOBAL TV. Her place at St Martins is pretty much booked for when she's old enough to go, if she can be bothered by then.

Crow's also designing her first high street collection for Miss Teen. Which keeps me busy too. I'm the one who picks up the phone, answers the emails, translates Crow's shoulders and makes sure everyone understands what she wants. I'm also learning the art of running a label. I've got extra-good at maths recently. Understanding Crow's finances is a lot harder than GCSE. What it basically comes down to, though, is that we owe Andy Elat a LOT of money.

The good side is that I get so much free fashion stuff now I can't even fit it all in my room. I keep some of it. A girl has to look good in this business. But the rest I give away to the charities that Edie supports to help Invisible Children return to normal life. They've already finished the new school. No need to call it after Henry. Instead, they called it after a friend of his, who died in the first raid.

Edie's been to see it. James and Grace looked after her when she visited Uganda. They're back at home, helping their community as they've always done. It took James a while to get used to this blonde teenager from Kensington trying to help out too. But she found Henry for him, so he can forgive a lot of Edie-ness. I'm absolutely certain she didn't do it for the CV points, but I bet the Harvard professors are going to be a lot more impressed with this than a video of Edie by a pool. She looks rubbish in a bikini anyway.

She's over in another corner, talking earnestly to Granny and the Director of the V&A and no doubt getting them to sign her petition. She's up to twenty thousand signatures now. She still looks as if she's dressed for tea at an embassy and there's nothing we can do to help her, but she doesn't seem to mind. She still hasn't decided about her fringe.

Jenny isn't here. She really meant it when she said she was going to keep her head down after the awards ceremonies. She's sick of parties, frocks and photographs and just wants to get on quietly with her GCSEs. She's doing French homework tonight, I think.

Harry's not here either. It's New York Fashion Week and he's gone over there to do the music for a couple of the big designers. After Crow's show so many of the models raved about him that he's got a bit of a waiting list and Mum has given up on him ever finishing his degree. At least it means he gets to see more of Svetlana, which both of them seem pretty happy about.

Henry, on the other hand, is standing quietly in a corner, reading a book of poems and waiting for Crow to finish so he can escort her home. Where Crow goes, Henry goes. That was clear from the start.

It turns out Henry *was* that boy they'd heard about in one of the camps, who wrote poems. He didn't talk, which was why no-one knew who he was. Nobody knew if he *could* talk. But when they asked him if he was Henry Lamogi and told him how much his family wanted him back, he simply said yes and he's been talking ever since.

Bad stuff happens, but every now and again miracles can happen too. (Although, admittedly, Edie helped. So did Andy Elat, with an emergency visa.) Life *can* be that kind.

Henry's hand occasionally moves to touch a long, jagged scar that runs from his cheek to the back of his head. It's the only visible sign of his experiences. Other than that, you'd assume he had always been the gentle student he is now. He's moved into a new flat with Florence and Crow while he catches up with his exams and it's hard to say who's looking after whom.

He can see Crow's tired and he's itching to take her away, but he won't say anything until she's ready. He's just a quiet, steady presence in her life, making sure she's OK.

I feel a movement behind us and realise that Mum has joined us. She puts a hand on my shoulder.

'What did Vivienne say?' I ask her.

'That the show was brilliant. But she also said it's a tough business. Hard work. Lots of disappointments. She's right. Are you sure you want it?'

Crow shrugs her shrug. She knows that if she wasn't a designer she'd go stark, staring bonkers. Thank goodness her dad understands.

I just laugh.

Me and Vivienne Westwood. Talking about the fashion business. La la la.

What you can do

If you want to show your compassion for children like Henry, Crow and Victoria, there are people out there helping and there is something you can do. The charities that I support are www.oxfam.org.uk and www.savethechildren.org.uk, but there are others doing a great job too. So ask your family and teachers, go online, find out more and do your bit to make a difference. Check out the Invisible Children campaign on www.invisiblechildren.com. Together, we can make good things happen.

Take fashion action like Edie. Why not join Save the Children's campaign?

Get all your friends to take action. You could win the chance to see how your action can save children's lives.

Save the Children is the world's independent children's charity. We're outraged that millions of children are still denied proper healthcare, food, education and protection. Save the Children are working flat out to secure the rights of children everywhere and we're determined to make further, faster changes. How many? How fast? It's up to you.

Visit **www.savethechildren.org.uk/threads**

Acknowledgements

Sitting down to write *Threads* in my local library, I had to imagine myself into lots of different worlds. I'd like to thank all the fashion bloggers, children's writing bloggers, the Invisible Children campaign and bloggers about life in the Ugandan displacement camps who helped me get where I needed to be. And whoever invented wifi.

Claire B. Shaeffer wrote a book called *Couture Sewing Techniques*. It was my couture bible and went with me everywhere (even though it's quite heavy).

Lola Gostelow is one of those people who works out how to make life better for children caught up in disasters round the world. I'm lucky to know her, and grateful for her advice, but anxious to stress that what I've written is partly fiction. Other people can describe the realities of life as a child soldier, displaced person or refugee better than me.

Katie Rhodes, Claire Potter and Anna Linwood read the first finished draft for me, when it was just a bunch of A4 papers in a blue folder. Their encouragement, and well-placed criticism, was exactly what I needed. If they ever feel like jobs as book critics, it's a career option.

The publication of this book was a fairy story in itself. And so I have to thank my own fairy godmothers: Barry Cunningham, Imogen Cooper, Rachel Hickman and the rest of the team at Chicken House. Their vision and passion has been my happy ever after.

I couldn't have created *Threads* without the help of all these wonderful people. Any mistakes and omissions are my own.

Want to know what happens next?

Can Crow find a winning idea for her new
high street collection?

Can Edie be sure that children aren't making
the clothes?

Will Jenny's new play be spoiled by the
Queen of Evil?

And why has Nonie's love life turned into
something from a horror movie?

Find out in summer 2010 in

*Threads
– The Second
Collection*

BY SOPHIA BENNETT

The fashion fairytale continues!

Now read on for an exclusive preview …

*C*row adores the Royal Opera House. She loves the thick red velvet curtains and the gold embroidery and the plush seats and the little girls with their mummies, all dressed up and on their best behaviour.

In their honour, she's worn a small set of pink fairy wings over her gold satin dungarees. And four purple velvet bows in her hair. It should look scary but she wears her clothes as if everyone dressed that way and, actually, she's gorgeous.

It seemed natural for Crow to use the other ticket. Edie has orchestra practice and Jenny's busy with the thing she's got to do with her playwright, whatever that is. And Crow enjoys the ballet more than them anyway. Yvette used to save up and bring her occasionally and she loves everything about it. The scenery, the costumes, the choreography, even the sound of the ballerinas' block shoes clicking across the floor when they do something complicated *en pointe.*

I love it too. Even when I'm not PERSONALLY INVITED by one of the dancers. Mum used to bring me when I was one of those little girls on their best behaviour. We used to sit at the back, because Mum liked to see the patterns made by the *corps de ballet*. And it's cheaper. It's where all the die-hard ballet fans sit, so you get to hear all the gossip about who's not dancing so well this week and who's about to get promoted.

But today, we're sitting in a box, at the side, right up close to the stage. Because I *have* been personally invited by one of the dancers and these are the tickets he left for me. You can practically hear the dancers breathe from here. It's weird. I'm not sure I wouldn't rather be at the back.

There are three short ballets tonight. Alexander is in the first and last. The opener is famous for its athletic jumping and I'm guessing he uses the middle one to get his breath back before lifting a bunch of ballerinas round the stage at the end.

As the curtain rises, Crow nudges me and hands me something – red opera glasses – so I can admire the dancers even more close up.

Goodness.

They really are very athletic. All of them. But Alexander most of all.

They don't muck about in the first ballet. They start as they mean to go on, with lots of leaping about everywhere and showing off their tights and their incredibly muscly legs. Alexander leaps beautifully. He takes off and then just seems to hang in midair for about twenty minutes, before landing delicately with a flourish and a smile. Then he whizzes round the stage doing pirouettes just to show how much energy he's still got.

My insides are pirouetting too. It seems that every third smile is aimed at our box and I'm guessing he's not directing them all at Crow, although she's certainly grinning at him fit to bust.

'He's amazing, isn't he?' she whispers cheerfully.

I nod. I'm not actually capable of speech right now. I can't really believe this is happening. Cute guy in the tights, the best dancer on the stage of the ROYAL OPERA HOUSE, is flirting with me FROM THE STAGE.

I must be dreaming. I keep waiting to wake up. But whenever I open my eyes, I'm still here, Crow's still grinning and Alexander is still rushing about, smiling straight at me whenever he's got a spare moment.

The first interval comes as a relief.

'Oh, by the way,' Crow says while we're queuing for ice creams. The Royal Opera House does the best ice creams in London, needless to say. 'Miss Teen want me to do another collection for next winter.'

WHAT?

'Sorry?' I mumble. 'I wasn't concentrating.'

So she says it again. The same words, in the same order.

Miss. Teen. Want. Her. To. Do. Another. Collection.

Goodness squared . . .

WIN THE CHANCE TO:

- experience a London Fashion Week show

- discover what it's like to work for a top Fashion PR company

Enter the THREADS fashion design and writing competition. Go to: **www.threadsthebook.com**

Fashion dreaming?

Plus, fabulous **free beauty stuff**; the latest THREADS **gossip**; meet **Sophia Bennett**; get **Nonie's** look or take fashion action like **Edie** …

www.threadsthebook.com